ALL THROUGH THE HOUSE

A Novel by
Joshua Millican

Based on a Screenplay by
Todd Nunes

Encyclopocalypse Publications
www.encyclopocalypse.com

ALL THROUGH THE HOUSE

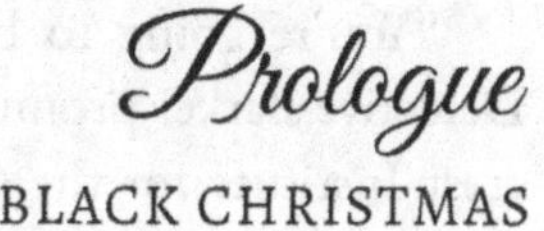

BLACK CHRISTMAS

Fifteen years ago...

"**Y**ou listen to me, you sick son of a bitch!"

Detective Barker seethes, staring at the piece of shit motherfucker sitting across the table from him in the interrogation room. Over his twenty years of service with the Napa Valley Police Department, he'd grown to loathe wife-beaters and child-molesters most of all. And didn't this poor excuse before him just take the cake.

"No more bullshit!" The detective rubs his left fist and clenches his teeth. "Confess!"

"I didn't do anything!"

Patrick Garrett's a mess: his hair tussled, his clothes torn, his face bruised and bleeding. He'd been manhandled by the arresting officers and humiliated during intake. He slumps against a wall, still in handcuffs, exhausted and overwhelmed, as the interrogator rages.

"We saw what you did to your child!" Detective Barker says. "Your own flesh and blood! How could you?"

"It was my wife!" Patrick says. "You gotta believe me!"

"Vivian told us everything!" Detective Barker shoots back, frustrated by the scumbag's obstinance. "Your obsession with... little girls and knives! You make me want to vomit!"

"No..."

"We've seen the pictures, and the masks, and the bags of dildos!"

"I don't know what you're talking about!" Patrick screams.

"You're going to be locked up for a long time, asshole," Detective Barker promises. "I'll make sure you land at the Readcrest Institute for the Criminally Insane. And when the other inmates find out you're a pedo-chomo who tried to throw his wife under the bus, well... your life will truly become a living hell."

"She'll pay for this!" Patrick says, his face a map of crazed, chaotic intent. "I'll kill that fucking psycho for doing this to me!"

Detective Barker meets the psychopath's smoldering gaze and laughs.

"When pigs fly."

Chapter One

SANTA CLAUS IS COMING TO TOWN

Every town has an Elm Street, but Spalding Road in Napa Valley, California is unique—and uniquely disturbing.

Built along the side of a ravine at the edge of dense woodlands, it feels more remote and isolated than it actually is, out of place and lost in time. It's a neighborhood of working-class family houses built in the 1940s, way past its prime.

The Christmas Season fails to bring winter cheer to this neck of the woods; rather, it accentuates the innate eeriness of the neighborhood like a false promise. The juxtaposition of expectations versus reality and the sweet stench of rotten nostalgia create an atmosphere of pervasive sadness. The residents of this lonely stretch have all been infected by it.

Stan, Kyle, and Eric are a trio of juvenile delinquents in training. Wrapped in winter jackets, they're prowling the neighborhood after midnight, committing petty acts of vandalism while sharing a single bottle of Miller Lite between them. Cars are egged, trees are toilet papered, bags of poop are alit on porches. It's all very naughty.

"Where should we go next?" Kyle asks, draining the last dregs of backwash from the beer bottle.

"I know!" Eric yells. "Let's go to the Creepy Christmas House!"

Stan and Kyle know exactly what he's talking about. Every kid in Napa County knows about the house that manages to somehow look scarier on Christmas than Halloween. It's legendary.

"I don't know," Stan says. "I heard the old lady who lives inside is a witch who likes to catch boys and cut their wieners off."

"Don't be stupid," Kyle replies. "I heard she's a black widow."

"She's a spider?" Stan's eyes are wide.

"No, stupid! A black widow is a lady serial killer who buries her dead husbands in the backyard."

"Quit being pussies, you guys," Eric chastises. "My mom says she's just a poor old lady. Let's go!"

The trio make their way down Spalding Road, passing other houses pointlessly decorated for the Holiday. Colorful lights blink and clink lightly in the wind, festive yet dreary wreaths adorn doors, plastic snowmen and reindeers populate front lawns.

It's not uncommon to see a life-sized Santa Claus on a front lawn. The more expensive models are animatronic; they wave, wishing passers-by a "Merry Christmas" with a "Ho-ho-ho!" in a jolly, electronic voice. Nothing strange about that.

The Creepy Christmas House at the end of the cul-de-sac, however, is very strange.

The lawn is literally packed with Santas: dozens of life-sized fat men in red suits, dozens of curly white beards swaying in the crisp wind, dozens of white pompoms dangling from the ends of pointed hats. Each one is slightly unique, varying in size, shape, dress or expression—all with dead, uncanny eyes.

The blue moonlight casts a chilling pallor over everything.

The sight's enough to cool the mischievous spirits of the troublesome trio wreaking havoc. They approach with caution.

"I don't know about this," Stan says uneasily, inching closer to the mob of plastic Santas.

"Yeah," Kyle agrees. "Maybe we should find another house to fuck with."

"Come on, you guys!" Eric's emphatic. "We came all the way up here! Now, I don't wanna leave until one of you hits one of those Santas in the head with a rock!"

Stan and Kyle look at each other and sigh. They know Eric will hound them relentlessly until he gets what he wants. The kid's a master at dispensing peer pressure.

"Okay, fine," Stan relents, bending down to pick up a fist-sized rock. "Which one do you want me to hit?"

The kids inspect the gaggle of Santas, looking for the perfect target.

"That one!" Eric points to a hunched monstrosity lurking in the periphery.

This Santa's a standout. His outfit's the same, but the mask is unique and sinister. Devoid of flesh-tones, the face is pitch black, blacker-than-black—almost like negative space, absorbing the light around it. It conveys an unsettling energy, like a cursed object or a blasphemous artifact. Primal, haunting, and down-right devilish.

"Jesus Christ!" Kyle exclaims. "Can you imagine if Santa Claus looked like that in real life?"

"Santa Claus isn't real, dillweed!" Eric says. "Grow up, Kyle."

Kyle rolls his eyes.

"I didn't mean... oh, never mind. Stan, throw the rock at that ugly Santa so we can get the hell out of here!"

Stan pulls his arm back, but hesitates.

"Do it!" Eric urges. "This is a poor person's house. My mom said it was okay."

"But what if I miss?" Stan asks. "What if I hit the window?"

"Who gives a shit?"

Even Kyle's getting impatient. "Throw it, you little bastard!"

"Fine!"

Stan, takes a deep breath, aims, and tosses the rock through the air with the precision of a major league baseball pitcher. It hits the black-faced Santa in the head with a satisfying crack!

Eric's thrilled. "You got it, Stan!"

The Santa wobbles on its base before falling over on the dead grass. A gust a wind hooks under the mask as it falls, pulling it from the mannequin's head. The mask lands face up, as though scowling at the world around it.

The boys erupt into a flurry of hoots and hollers.

"Do it again!" Eric says.

"Okay!"

As Stan reaches down for another rock, the front door of the house swings open. Mrs. Garrett, a stern middle-aged woman wearing a Christmas-themed bathrobe, emerges in a fluster.

"What the hell's going on out here?" she calls out.

While the woman isn't physically imposing, the intensity of her anger startles the boys. They jump back and scatter.

"It's the witch!" Eric screams. "Run!"

The boys retreat into the shadows as a sudden gust pushes down from the west, howling. The trees sway in the wind, shedding the last of their autumn leaves. Mrs. Garrett shivers, pulling her bathrobe tighter around her before heading back inside.

"Naughty boys," she mutters, closing the door and locking it behind her.

The porch light goes out and the neighborhood goes quiet. The boys are gone and Mrs. Garrett heads back to bed. But the street isn't empty.

Someone's been watching from the gloom. A shuffling hulk

emerges from the darkness with shoulders slumped; his long, greasy hair completely covers his face. He seems to heave with every breath, expanding and contracting beneath the moonlight.

His nondescript, standardized clothing suggests he's recently escaped from a prison or an insane asylum. The blood-splatter staining him head-to-toe suggests the escape was a violent one—with many casualties. The fugitive reaches into his pocket and retrieves a piece of paper: his Naughty List.

The hulk looks up at the Creepy Christmas House and hisses. He sheds his bloodied clothing and strips the toppled Santa Claus mannequin. The red and white suit's a perfect fit for the shape, and warmer than his discarded scrubs. He spots the bizarre Santa mask with the blacker-than-black face and picks it up curiously.

Put me on, the ghoulish mask beckons, like a tempting demon. *Put me on, and we'll show this town a bloodbath beyond imagination. Put me on and have your vengeance!*

The mask fits his head like a glove, like a second skin. It seems to sharpen his hearing, his eyesight, and his resolve. He'd been a quivering mass of wrath; now he's focused, fiendish—and furious!

A light goes out on the second story of the Creepy Christmas House, indicating Mrs. Garrett's gone back to bed. The newly adorned Santa decides he'll deal with her tomorrow. Besides, there are plenty of names on the Naughty List to keep him occupied.

Like Sheila Davenport.

The bad Santa turns to head down Spalding Road. He spots a rusty set of twelve-inch gardening shears sticking out of Mrs. Garrett's lawn.

He snatches them up.

Don't forget to grab your sack, the evil mask reminds him.

Chapter Two

LITTLE DRUMMER BOY

Five-year-old Jacob Davenport wakes up in his mother's bed, snuggled in his mother's arms.

Someone's knocking at the door.

The boy sits up and rubs his eyes.

"Mom?" Jacob shakes his mother gently at first, then with a bit more force. She continues snoring softly, completely undisturbed.

She passed out after drinking a few beers and a box of cheap wine. She was too wasted to change out of the stripper clothes she's been wearing since the end of her last shift. Jacob could clobber her with a sledgehammer and she probably wouldn't flinch.

The knocking continues.

"Mom, there's someone at the door."

Nothing in response.

The boy sighs and slips out of bed, immediately kicking over a few empty beer bottles. The room's in a state of disarray. A string of white Christmas lights framing the window offers little warmth. Jacob sidesteps pizza boxes and piles of dirty clothes as he makes his way towards the living room.

He approaches the front door, yawning, as the knocking continues, getting louder—impatient.

"Dad?" the boy calls out. "Is that you? Are you locked out?"

There's a short pause before the knocking starts up again even louder—frantic.

Jacob gasps softly. He darts over to the front window, pulls back the curtain, and takes a peek. The porch light has been out for months. Still, beneath the moonlight, the boy sees a familiar figure.

"Santa?" His eyes open wide with excitement. Mom and Dad already told him there wouldn't be enough money for presents this year (just like last year and every year since he was born). But he'd written a letter to Santa Claus, addressed it to The North Pole, and dropped it into a mailbox on a lark. Santa must have gotten it!

"Santa" sees Jacob peeking through the window and takes pause.

The mask senses his hesitation.

What's the matter? it whispers.

He wasn't exactly sane when he was put away. Still, years of incarceration and systematic abuse have transformed this lost soul into an abysmal monstrosity. His humanity's withered into nothingness, and the black-as-the-void mask fills the empty space with the most despicable of urges.

You know what you have to do. Tuck him in and say Goodnight.

Santa cocks his head and waves at Jacob, his rusty shears hidden behind his back.

Chapter Three

SHEILA DAVENPORT AND ADELE COOPER

Sheila jerks up in bed, screaming. She's just had a terrible nightmare about a gang of gray aliens with long probing fingers—chasing her. Taking a moment to compose herself, she grabs a cigarette off the nightstand and lights it. Soon, the vivid details of her dream dissipate like steam into nothingness.

It's the middle of the night and she's already hung the fuck over. She rubs her throbbing temples and groans. She's been working day shifts at the Hot Beaver Strip Club outside Petaluma and drinking away her indignations every night.

Things were easier when her boyfriend/co-parent Adele was around to help carry the load. But he's been gone since the beginning of harvest season, working on a guerrilla cannabis farm in Mendocino. He promised to make it home in time for Christmas, but Sheila isn't holding her breath.

Life has been hard, full of disappointment and disillusionment, and Sheila hasn't always faced her problems head-on. But she's never forgotten her true reason for being; the light of her dismal life, her precious son Jacob.

But where is he?

"Jacob?" He's been sleeping in her bed with her ever since the space-heater in his room crapped out. "Jacob, buddy?" she calls again. "Where are you?"

No response.

Sheila huffs and hops out of bed. Off-kilter and annoyed, she wobbles out of her room and down the hall. The house is unusually cold.

She stops in her tracks when she gets to the living room, seeing the front door is wide open. A frigid blast slaps Sheila's face and barely-covered body like an unruly drunk. She sees a chair pushed up beside the doorframe, indicating Jacob had hoisted himself up to unfasten the deadbolt.

She sobers up—fast.

"Jacob? Are you outside?" Sheila takes a few anxious steps towards the door and looks out. The cheap plastic Christmas decorations on her lawn have been mangled. "Those little bastards," she mutters, silently cursing the neighborhood's pubescent hoodlums. She scans up and down the street, but not a creature is stirring.

Sheila shuts and locks the front door before rushing back into the living room.

"Jacob!" She's on the verge of turning frantic when she notices her son sleeping on the couch, wrapped in his Frosty the Snowman blanket. Beside him, an aluminum Christmas tree wrapped in blue lights blinks festively.

She's overcome with relief and sighs, tension leaving her body.

"You little shit." She lingers beside him and smiles. "At least someone around here can sleep."

Sheila runs her fingers through his curly locks and kisses his forehead. She loves him so much it hurts.

"Love you, Mommy," the little boy murmurs from a dream-state.

She starts heading back to her bedroom, but decides she

won't be able to get back to sleep. She feels disgusting, frankly; sweaty and smokey with the scent of cheap alcohol wafting from her pores.

"I need a shower," she says out loud to no one as she walks into the bathroom.

Sheila stands before the mirror and lights a couple of candles. She prefers this soft light to the bright flickering fluorescents overhead. She examines her face, her hair, and her teeth before turning to the bathtub and running the faucet. Soon, warm water's streaming from the shower head, filling the room with mist.

She doesn't notice the dark figure lurking behind the bathroom door, clutching rusty gardening shears.

Sheila slips off her bra and thong before stepping into the shower. Hot water soothes as fragrant steam wraps around her like a hug. She uses an exfoliating sponge and scented moisturizer to lather her body. Her headache dissolves; the muscles in her neck loosen and pop. It's bliss.

She doesn't hear the door creaking open or the footsteps approaching her—until it's too late.

Sheila freezes as the shower curtain is viciously yanked back. She screams when she sees a man standing over her. Her blood boils, however, when she realizes it's her boyfriend, Adele.

"Surprise!"

"Jesus Christ, Adele!" Sheila slaps him with both hands, splashing him with sudsy water. "You just about scared me to death!"

He cools her temper with a passionate kiss. Their mouths open, their tongues reunite, their libidos flare.

"I've been missing you, Adele," Sheila says sweetly.

"I missed you too, baby," Adele replies. "I'm about to show you just how much!" He strips off his shirt and begins unfastening his belt.

Sheila bites her bottom lip.

"Is he big already?" she asks, peering down at Adele's crotch.

"It's been a long drive, baby," he replies. "But don't worry. He'll get there." He pulls out his dick, practically moving into the shower.

But Sheila pushes him away.

"Stop," she says. "You know I hate seeing him when... he isn't happy. He looks like a dead sea cucumber!"

"He'll get happy, Sheila. Just give him a second, and he'll be gleaming with Christmas joy."

Sheila remains unconvinced.

"Why don't you go to my room and get him ready," she suggests seductively, caressing her breasts. "I'll be there in a second."

"Don't take long," Adele replies with a huff. "I'm about to blast that pussy into next week!"

He heads to the bedroom in order to prepare himself, leaving his lover alone again. Once in Sheila's messy bedroom, he gets down to business. He starts stroking, softly at first; but it isn't long before his pace becomes feverish.

"Come on, Boy!" he pleads. "Don't let me down now. Let's do this. Let the sun shine in..."

Santa, still camouflaged within shadows and the low lighting of the bathroom, silently moves into position.

Sheila finishes rinsing her hair and washing her body. She turns the shower water off. She pulls the curtain back... and her blood—freezes! Her face becomes a contortion of horror.

Eyes inside a mask stare at Sheila, flaring with icy treachery. Santa opens his rusty shears, heaving with every breath. Without hesitation, he plunges a blade into one of Shiela's money-makers, impaling her perfect left breast.

Sheila looks down at her mutilated body, watching her life draining out of her. Blood begins to fill the tub, swirling down the drain.

The blade slips out as Sheila falls back into the shower. More of her blood sprays across the white tile walls. She gurgles, struggling to speak, staring up at her killer.

He doesn't like the way she's looking at him, so he plunges the gardening shears deep into her eyes. Sheila's final breath escapes with a squeak.

Good work! The black mask praises the killer. *You're a natural!*

The slaying Santa beams with pride.

Now, the mask commands in a voice only its wearer can hear, *let's finish this!*

The bearded brute heads down the hall to Sheila's bedroom.

Adele, his back to the door, thinks he hears Sheila returning from her shower.

"Almost there, baby," Adele promises while stroking. "Oh yeah! That's right, Buddy. Get strong for me!" He hears footsteps behind him. "Get on the bed, Sexy. Mr. Happy's comin' to town!" He can sense a warm body standing right behind him, mere inches away. "Choke on this, baby!" He spins, coming face to face with pure evil—a visage blacker than midnight.

The butcher opens his shears.

Adele's paralyzed with dread; his erection remains at full attention.

The butcher sneers; his mind spins. He can't help but focus on Adele's throbbing member. It represents everything he's missing, everything that was ripped away from him, a lifetime of torment.

Take it from him! the mask hisses.

Adele's eyes bulge in fear as the rusty blades sever Mr. Happy; his penis falls to the floor, seemingly in slow motion. Blood gushes down both of his legs. The pain is enough to snap him back from his temporary paralysis.

He screams in agony.

Chapter Four

PRESENTS FOR CHRISTMAS

I t's getting dark.

Rachel Kimmel drives her white Toyota up Spalding Road, past the pointless spectacles of lights and lawn ornaments, past the crumbling homes with sad threads of gray smoke leaking from chimneys.

She wonders why anyone even bothers anymore. *This has to be least "merry" street in all of Napa*, she thinks.

She has a love/hate relationship with Christmas. Fifteen years ago, during the Christmas Season, her life was completely shattered. It was one of those events that divides a life into before and after. She was barely five at the time, but she remembers it like it was yesterday.

"Take me with you!" young Rachel pleads, pulling on her mother's sweater. "Please!"

"I can't take you with me right now, Bunny," her mother replies while getting into the front seat of her car, looking desperate.

"I don't understand!" Young Rachel weeps as the cloudy sky above unleashes rain.

Her mom closes the door and rolls down the window.

"I'll explain everything," she tells her daughter before starting the car. "I promise, Bunny, I'll tell you everything. About tonight, about your father. No more secrets, I promise. But if I don't leave right now, something very bad might happen!"

"When will you come back?"

"Just stay at your grandma's house and I'll be home by Christmas." She turns on the windshield wipers as the rain intensifies. "I promise, Bunny."

"You swear?"

"I swear!"

That was the last time she, or anyone else, had seen Laura Kimmel.

It was the same night that all of the infamous commotion took place at the Garrett House up the street, but young Rachel hardly noticed. She spent the night on the bed in her grandmother's guest room, lying in the fetal position, wrapped in a blanket. Her sorrow was devastating.

Rachel suppresses tears as she nears her destination. It's been almost a year since she left to attend UC Santa Cruz and, at first, she wasn't sure she wanted to come back. But Christmas is near, and the season pulls on her heartstrings. It feels like a physical force, like the gravity of Planet X—unseen yet undeniable. She simply can't stay away.

Even though she hates Christmas, the trauma it stirs, the inevitable disappointment it creates, she just can't leave it all behind. She still has hope; hope that her mother will keep her promise and arrive at her grandma's house on Christmas morning. Hope that she'll finally have answers to the questions that dog her like phantoms. Hope that she'll finally feel... whole again.

Rachel pulls up in front of her grandmother's house, puts her car in park, and kills the ignition. She braces herself for the reunion since the two of them didn't leave things on the best of terms. *I wonder if she'll even be happy to see me*, she ponders.

When Rachel's mother disappeared, her grandmother Abbey took her in without hesitation. She cleaned up her hard partying lifestyle and prepared to be a parent again. Abbey never sought to replace Rachel's mother; she simply did the best she could.

And Rachel adored her for it. When Abbey was injured in an accident, Rachel took a year off school to nurse her back to health. And though Rachel was happy to do it, the situation made her feel stuck—and the idea of being tied to this small town forever terrified her.

Rachel had left suddenly, deciding a clean break was necessary. No one even knew she'd been applying to colleges until the day she left.

"Just get it over with," Rachel mutters to herself, taking off her seatbelt. She exits the car and goes around to the back in order to retrieve her overstuffed backpack and a single present. When she closes the trunk, she notices some hubbub up the road.

At the end of the cul-de-sac, Rachel spots an unmarked police car, a single red beacon light spinning atop it, parked by the old Garrett House (the place the kids still call the Creepy Christmas House). She sees an older cop in a trenchcoat talking to someone.

Detective Barker's in his late-fifties and just a few weeks shy of retirement. He's got a stern look on his face and suspicious eyes. Rachel can only catch bits of what he's saying.

"...broke out late last night... canvasing the neighborhood... call us if you hear anything!"

As Rachel heads up the walkway to her grandmother's house, she sees the cop is talking to Mrs. Garrett.

"Oh my," she replies to the detective.

Rachel can hardly believe her eyes. She hasn't seen Mrs. Garrett in fifteen years—no one has. After that terrible night, she retreated inside her home and rarely emerged. She looks just like Rachel remembered, but older, of course, and more severe.

"Thank you so much for stopping by, Detective," Mrs. Garrett says.

The cop prattles on a bit.

Mrs. Garrett listens to Detective Barker intently, until she notices Rachel. She breaks eye contact with the cop and gives Rachel a huge, enthusiastic wave. The smile on her face seems exaggerated, almost plastic.

Rachel waves back listlessly, noticing that Mrs. Garrett is in the process of adding even more Christmas décor to her overstuffed lawn. *Maybe she's going for a world record*, she thinks. Rachel turns back to the house and takes a deep breath before letting herself in.

Rachel enters a modest yet cozy home, all decked in the Christmas spirt; there's an inviting blaze in the fireplace and a colorful tree covered in lights and tinsel. She drops her backpack by the door and walks closer to the tree, clutching the present. She's inundated with childhood memories from before her mother disappeared, and she smiles.

"Grandma..." she announces. "I'm home."

She looks down at the gift in her hand. A tag reads, *"For Mom."* She leans down and places it under the tree—just as she's done every season for the past fifteen years. *Maybe this year...* but she can't even complete the thought.

A crackling voice comes up behind her.

"What do you think you're doing?"

Rachel turns. "Hi, Grandma!"

Rachel's grandmother, Abbey Kimmel, is a firecracker of a

septuagenarian with long, white hair. She broke her hip when a drunk driver crashed into her a few years back and has been confined to a wheelchair ever since. You'd hardly know it, though; Abbey seems just as able-bodied and spry as ever.

Rachel beams at Abbey and leans down to give her a hug.

"I'm so sorry I haven't returned your calls."

The tension between them evaporates, replaced by genuine love and affection.

"Well, you're a big girl now," Abbey replies. "If you want to leave your past behind, that's your prerogative."

"I'd never leave you behind, Grandma," Rachel says sweetly.

Abbey notices the present Rachel left under the Christmas tree for her mother and clucks her tongue.

"I hoped you'd finally stopped leaving presents for your mother." Her voice conveys more than a hint of disappointment. "I don't think holding out hope all of these years has done you a lick of good. You had the right idea when you left this town in the rearview mirror. It's time to get on with your life."

"It's my Christmas tradition," Rachel explains. "I have to."

"No, you don't," is Abbey's stern reply. "It was cute when you were a kid, but now it's getting downright creepy. Move on, Rachel."

Rachel holds her grandmother's hand and presses the conversation.

"Maybe I could if I didn't have so many unanswered questions." Rachel takes a seat on the couch. "You never tell me anything, Grandma, and my mother promised to explain everything just as soon as she got back. I'm still waiting. I need that explanation!"

"Wouldn't change a damn thing," Abbey replies, crossing her arms over her chest. "I could never control your mother. She was a free spirit. I hoped she'd finally settle down once you came along. For a while, it looked like she might. But pulling up stakes and leaving town without telling anyone is exactly the kind of thing she'd do."

Rachel knows it's pointless to argue. Her grandmother is stubborn as a mule, always has been. Rachel wonders if Abbey even knows what happened to her daughter, or if she's in the dark just like everyone else. Either way, Rachel hopes for a peaceful, stress-free holiday. She lets it go, for now.

"I'm so happy to see you, Grandma."

Abbey softens and smiles. "I'm so happy to see you too, Rachel. Can I get you something to eat? You must be starving."

"No, thank you," Rachel replies. "I just stopped by to drop off my bag. I promised Gia and Sarah we'd all go Christmas shopping tonight. But we can spend the entire day together tomorrow, I promise."

"Fine by me," Abbey says. "I've got a huge bridge tournament tonight and I plan on kicking some ass." Abbey flexes her eyebrows. "Oh, I just remembered something!" Abbey wheels off to the kitchen and returns with a Christmas Card in a bright red envelope addressed to Rachel. "This arrived for you the other day. What great timing!"

Rachel looks at the envelope and furrows her brow. There's no return address. "Hmm, I wonder who this is from?"

"Well open it up and find out," Abbey says.

Rachel tears into the envelope and opens the festive card, adorned with boughs of holly. The smile on her face drops when she sees who sent it.

"This is from... Mrs. Garrett."

Abbey looks up, concerned. "That's strange," she says.

"I just saw her when I was pulling up, actually," Rachel says. "She was talking to some sort of cop. How weird."

Abbey shakes her head.

"There's definitely something weird about that lady. What the hell does she say?"

Rachel finishes reading and a strange, quizzical look washes over her face.

"She wants to know if I'll help decorate her house for Christmas."

"Now I've heard everything!" Abbey says with a humph. "Who the hell does shit like that? Asking a random neighbor to decorate your house." She looks out the window and up at the old house at the end of the cul-de-sac. "Decorate your own house, you old bat!" Abbey tuns back to her granddaughter. "She hasn't stepped foot out of that house for fifteen years and now, suddenly, she wants to be your best friend?"

"She's offering to pay me," Rachel interjects. "Tuition in California isn't cheap—even at State universities."

"I don't give a hoot if she's Mama Warbucks. I say, 'Fuck her!'"

Rachel laughs at her grandmother's foul mouth. "Language," she scolds. "Besides, it's Christmas. Don't you even feel a little sorry for her? I mean, considering what happened to her husband and her daughter... all the rumors and isolation. It couldn't have been easy."

"That was a long time ago," Abbey replies with little sympathy. "As far as I'm concerned... it's none of our damn business."

Rachel sighs. "I can't even think about this right now." She stuffs the card into her jacket pocket. "We can talk more about it when I get back home tonight." She grabs her purse and heads out the front door. "I love you, Grandma."

Abbey smiles back.

"I love you too, sweetheart. Have fun with your friends."

Abbey's smile fades as soon as Rachel's out the door. She looks back out the window and up towards the ominous house against the edge of the woods.

"What are you up to, you crazy old witch?" she sneers.

Chapter Five

FROSTY

Rachel walks towards her car. The cold winter air envelopes her, and she shivers. She looks down the way and sees that Mrs. Garrett has gone back inside.

The weird old cop, however, is still there, leaning against his car, smoking a cigarette.

He waves at her.

"Happy Holidays," he says.

"Thank you?" she replies uncertainly. She doesn't much like police officers. She remembers feeling like the entire lot of them were useless back when her mother disappeared.

"I'd wish you a Merry Christmas, but that might get me lynched!" He guffaws, walking closer to her. "You look like one of those woke feminist types."

"Whatever," Rachel responds dismissively, unlocking her car door.

He introduces himself, approaching Rachel with his hand outstretched.

"I'm Detective William Barker."

Rachel reluctantly shakes his hand.

"Rachel Kimmel," she responds, coldly.

"Rachel Kimmel," he repeats. "Why, I remember you from back when you were just a sprout. Shame about your mother."

Rachel shoots him a look with daggers. *It's a shame you guys are useless*, she thinks. "Yeah, whatever."

"Well, I can see you're on your way out, so I won't keep you long." Detective Barker drops his cigarette and stamps it out with his foot. "But there's been some trouble over the past few nights. People have reported a prowler dressed like Santa Claus."

Rachel smirks. "Perfect disguise for this time of year, I guess."

"Well, aren't you clever." He reaches into his jacket pocket, grabs a fresh cigarette, and lights it. "Like I said, I won't keep you. Just wanted to ask if you've noticed anything... unusual?"

"Like?"

"It seems there was a bit of commotion on Spalding Road last night. Did you see or hear anything?"

Rachel figures this must be what he and Mrs. Garrett were discussing earlier.

"I've been gone for a while," she replies. "I just got in a few hours ago."

"Well, welcome home!" the detective replies jovially. "Have a nice evening. Be safe out there, and don't hesitate to call us if you notice anything... unusual."

"Sure." As Rachel opens her car door, she notices Mrs. Garrett coming back outside—maneuvering yet another life-sized Santa Claus mannequin.

Detective Barker notices Rachel noticing Mrs. Garrett.

"How well do you know Mrs. Garrett?" he asks.

Rachel's slightly taken aback by the change of subject.

"Not very well," she replies. "She's lived next door to my grandma all my life, but we're not close."

"Hmm." Detective Barker seems curious, but also calculating, like a poker player. "Did you know her husband?"

"I can't remember much."

"Well…" The detective hesitates. "Do you know what happened to him?"

"Just the rumors," Rachel replies. "He was violent and sick so he was arrested and locked-up."

Detective Barker chuckles.

"'Sick' is a mild way of putting it. We put him away at the Readcrest Institute for the Criminally Insane. When the other inmates got ahold of him, they cut off his dick and flushed it down the toilet."

Rachel's momentarily shocked and repulsed, and Barker notices.

"Sorry," he says. "I hope I didn't offend your delicate sensibilities."

Rachel shakes her head and sneers. "My sensibilities aren't delicate. I just find you somewhat crude."

He shrugs his shoulders. "Funny, I've heard that before. Well, I won't keep you. Be careful tonight, won't you? Like I was saying… prowler and whatnot…" He retreats to his car, waving goodbye.

"Yeah, sure," Rachel replies, stepping into her car.

"One more thing." Detective Barker turns around. "Did you know the child?"

"Jamie?" Rachel asks, remembering Mr. and Mrs. Garrett's daughter. "When we were kids, we'd see her in the window sometimes. She was never allowed to come out and play. Didn't she disappear right around the time Mr. Garrett went away?"

"More or less," Barker replies without elaborating. "Bye now," he says without leaving.

There's a loud clatter up the street. Mrs. Garrett is having a hell of a time with her latest Santa Claus. It's fallen over and it looks like she and the mannequin are wrestling on her front porch.

Rachel sighs. "She asked me to help her with her decorations," she tells the detective. "I should probably go and give her a hand."

"Well, that's quite neighborly of you," Barker replies with a hint of sarcasm.

"She's just a poor old lady. It must have been hard for her, losing her husband and daughter at the same time."

"I used to think she was just a poor old lady, too," Barker says. "Now... I'm not so sure."

Rachel rolls her eyes. *Typical cop bullshit*, she thinks, as she starts walking toward Mrs. Garrett.

"It was lovely chatting with you, Ms. Kimmel." Detective Barker turns towards his vehicle one last time. "Please do be in touch." He finally gets into his car and drives away, flicking his cigarette out the window while speeding off.

Fat chance, Rachel thinks.

Chapter Six

FOR GOODNESS SAKE

Rachel approaches as Mrs. Garrett manages to set her latest Santa mannequin upright.

"Oof!" She's sweaty and flustered. She grabs the Santa around the waist and heaves but loses her balance and stumbles.

"I got it!" Rachel calls, rushing forward.

"Rachel Kimmel, it's wonderful to see you!" Mrs. Garrett perks up and looks delighted. "Thank you, dear!"

Rachel grabs one end of the Santa, then she and Mrs. Garrett work together to bring the Santa out. They stand him up with his brethren and admire him.

"Oh my!" Mrs. Garrett collects herself and straightens her hair. "I thought Santa and I were goners for a second. Thank goodness you came along."

"It is Christmas, after all," Rachel replies. "Be good for goodness' sake, and all that."

Mrs. Garrett smiles wide and gives Rachel a warm, friendly hug. She has a pungent scent, like mothballs, ointments, and arthritis cream. Her face is caked with foundation, ineffectually covering the wrinkles around her eyes and on her forehead.

"Rachel Kimmell... I'm so happy you came by. There's just no way I could decorate this house all by myself."

What have I gotten myself into? Rachel thinks. *Gia and Sarah are gonna kill me if I'm late!*

"Well, actually..." Rachel pauses, attempting to figure out how to extricate herself from this situation. But there's nothing she can say, really. Not without sounding like a total grinch—at Christmas time. She resigns herself. Maybe it'll be quick. She sighs. "How can I help?"

"I just need some decorations brought down from the attic and some lights put up inside," Mrs. Garrett says with a coy smile. "This year is really important to me... I have a very special guest coming for Christmas and I want everything to be perfect."

Rachel sees a sparkle in Mrs. Garrett's eyes. Her heart warms.

"It really looks like you're getting your life back together," Rachel says. "I'm really happy for you. I can't imagine how difficult it must have been..." she chooses her words carefully, "losing your family."

Mrs. Garrett's eyelids flutter, but her smile never falters.

"I can't hide in this house forever," the old lady replies.

"You're doing the right thing," Rachel assures her. "Trust me. I'm still working on letting my mother go, so I know how hard it is."

Mrs. Garrett's eyes brighten.

"It's comforting to talk with someone who understands," she replies. "Despite our ages, we actually have a lot in common. Do you remember Jamie from when you were little?"

Rachel furrows her brow as distant memories come back into focus. She remembers the strange, sad girl who looked down at her longingly from her bedroom window.

Many of the kids were cruel. They would taunt the poor girl in the window. They would throw nasty things at the glass and call her hurtful names. Crude boys would flash their wieners and their butts. Rachel's heart aches when she imagines how the young girl must have felt.

"I remember Jamie couldn't play outside," Rachel says. "She had some kind of skin disease, didn't she?

"Yes," Mrs. Garrett replies. "It's called Bowen's Disease. She had burning patches of red scaly skin all over her body, poor thing. It was on her scalp too, so I couldn't even brush her hair. But she was the light of my life." The old lady pauses, becoming morose. "I was never the same once she was taken from me. It's a shame. With the right treatment, she could've been like you: in college... beautiful..." She begins to lose herself in recollections.

"I have painful memories too," Rachel says in a soothing voice. "I try not to dwell too much on them, but I understand how hard it can be to... move on from the past"

"I didn't know your mother very well," Mrs. Garrett replies, clumsily changing the topic again. "But I remember how beautiful she was. In fact, when I saw you earlier, that was the first thing I thought of. You two look so much alike."

"Really?" Rachel's taken aback, stunned and flattered. "You really think I look like her?"

Mrs. Garrett nods and smiles. "Would you like to come in for something to drink before we get started?"

"Oh, right... decorating." Lost in a sudden tidal wave of recollections, Rachel almost forgot all about her friends. "I have to go shopping now, but I shouldn't be more than a couple of hours. Can I come back and help you then?"

"Heaven's yes!" Mrs. Garrett looks elated. "I'll take whatever help I can get."

"Ok, great," Rachel replies. "I'll see you later tonight."

Mrs. Garrett watches Rachel walk away, her eyes narrowing ever so slightly.

"See you soon," she says.

At the edge of the woods, a dark figure has been lurking in the shadows.

See you soon, the evil mask echoes.

Chapter Seven

KISSING SANTA CLAUS

At first glance, the interior of the Garrett House looks like a Norman Rockwell painting. The atmosphere pulses with a warm amber glow. A Victorian Christmas Tree features prominently in the living room, dozens of wrapped presents at its base. There's a crackling fire in the fireplace; stockings have been hung by the chimney with care. The halls are decked with boughs of holly, jingling bells, and mistletoe.

It's only when taking the long view of the Garrett House that its uncanniness becomes apparent. Though the living room is picturesque, there are at least as many Santas inside as there are on the front lawn. Dozens of mannequins—maybe a hundred.

There are Santas in the dining room, in the halls, stuffed into bedrooms and bathrooms and closets. Each Santa is slightly unique; many are in various stages of decomposition and decay. Some look sick, others decrepit. Some hardly look human. All of them have dead eyes.

Mrs. Garrett's standing by the door to the master suite, screaming at someone within.

"Stop telling me what to do!" She's furious. "I'm not just

some punching bag that you can take your aggression out on whenever you want. You men are all the same! You only care about one thing and it doesn't matter who you hurt!" Her hands are balled into fists; her face is red and the tendons in her neck are flexing.

No one responds.

"And don't think that I've forgotten what you did to me," she continues, spittle flying from her mouth. "You're nothing but a perverted monster! I was just a child and you passed me around to all those men like I wasn't even human!"

She's been screaming at one of her Santa Claus mannequins.

"How can you call yourself a father?"

Mrs. Garrett's expression changes abruptly and she recoils. Her sad, angry eyes fill with disbelief. The Santa Claus mannequin seems... angry.

His forehead furrows, his eyes turn bloodshot, and he seems to be breathing.

Mrs. Garrett's mouth falls open in horror.

"It can't be..." she whispers.

He's alive!

"I've had enough of your fat mouth!" Santa screams, pouncing.

They tumble to the ground and wrestle down the hallway. Santa gets the upper hand, straddling Mrs. Garrett and wrapping his gloved hands around her neck. He squeezes with inhuman force.

Mrs. Garrett's jaw unhinges, her hair stands on end, her eyes bug out of her skull. She tries to scream but she can't—

She jerks awake on the sofa, panicked and panting.

She'd fallen asleep while knitting.

"Oh my!" she gasps. "What a nightmare!" She begins to relax, collecting herself as fear subsides.

These dreams are nothing new. Santa Claus, her father, her husband: they combined into a perfect storm for burgeoning psychosis. Over the years, her memories had merged into a supervillain, relentlessly stalking her subconscious.

"Stay away from men, Vivian," she remembers her mother telling her when she was just a kid, a vicious look on her face. "They only want one thing, and they don't care who they hurt. Beware the purple snake, Vivian!"

"Yes, Mama," meek little Vivian replies.

Her mother always used to say, "The only man you can trust is Santa Claus!"

At the time, little Vivian didn't realize that her mother was being facetious—that it was a joke. She still thought Santa Claus was real. But ever since she was a child, whenever men scared her into solitude or sent her reeling, she imagined kindly Santa Claus, the only man she could ever truly trust, taking her away from her life of despondency.

Every Christmas, as a child, she would sit on Santa's lap at the mall. She would bury her face in his beard, silently weeping, wishing he would whisk her off to the North Pole to live happily ever after. The scene played out year after year, even after she learned that Santa Claus wasn't real—even after she grew too old to sit on Santa's Lap.

When she was thirteen, the mall Santa tutted her. "Aren't you a little old for this?"

She was. As much as she feared men and loved Santa, she wanted more than a concept, more than a myth. She wanted a physical connection; arms and a body. Any sensation remotely resembling desire filled her with blistering shame.

She wandered through the mall in a daze, conflicting emotions twisting inside her.

On her way out, she passed the Christmas display in Macy's. A mannequin Santa was surrounded by elves, a sack of presents slung over his shoulder. His smile, though artificial, was also genuine. The sensations in her body were tempestuous.

"I love you, Santa," she whispered. Slightly self-aware, she looked around uneasily; the other customers and salespeople were distracted by their own endeavors. So, as a burgeoning fetishist, she made her move.

She stepped into the display and wrapped her arms around Santa. She put her head against his chest and buried her face in his beard. This Santa didn't think she was too young *or* too old. This Santa thought she was perfect.

As though in a trance, she let her right hand explore the mannequin thoroughly, eventually venturing into his baggy red slacks. She gasped and trembled.

This Santa didn't have a purple snake. This Santa was smooth to the touch. Young Vivian's eyes widened. Maybe Santa *was* the perfect man after all; a protector, a provider... a eunuch.

Later, after Jamie was born, she had hoped her husband, Peter, would leave her alone They had their perfect child and she no longer considered sex a necessity. Peter, however, made it clear that "shit doesn't work that way."

"Men have needs," he'd say.

She knew all about men and their disgusting needs.

Thus began a carnal cold war that lasted years. There were negotiations and attempts at treaties. Mrs. Garrett thought sex might be tolerable if Peter wore a Santa Claus suit, long white beard and all. It worked for a while; Peter was satisfied, but she wasn't. She wished Peter could be smooth—like the mannequin at Macy's. Santa with actual man-parts felt like a corruption of her idealized archetype, her beloved soulmate.

She felt so incredibly alone once Peter and Jamie were both gone. That's when she started her collection, eventually assembling a veritable legion of Santas. They would never hurt her or make her feel dirty—and they would never leave her.

But they weren't enough to keep the nightmares at bay.

Mrs. Garrett gets up from the sofa and heads into the guest room.

"Hello, darling!" She greets the only female mannequin in

the house, a striking beauty with red lips and long dark hair. It's dressed in an elegant sequin gown and surrounded by a plethora of red poinsettia. "Don't worry," she says while stroking the mannequin's cheek. "I'll never let them hurt you the way they hurt me."

The mannequin wears a gold necklace with an engraved charm. It reads: "*Daughter*."

The mannequin looks a lot like Rachel.

Chapter Eight

SANTA LOOKS A LOT LIKE DADDY

Rachel pulls her car into Gia Remmy's driveway and honks the horn. Gia comes bounding out of her house and hops in the car. She's boisterous and stylish with rosy cheeks and a fantastic smile.

The young women hug each other, squealing with delight.

"I've missed you so much!" Gia says, releasing her hug and beaming at her bestie. "This boring town is awful without you."

"I can't believe a part of me actually missed this place," Rachel replies. "I feel like I've been gone for years."

"Let's not waste any time!" Gia claps her hands together. "I've got my daddy's Gold Card and the shops stay open late. Let's hit it!"

As the car pulls out, neither notices the stalking Santa standing close by. He blends into the scenery.

"Look at these beautiful Cornelia James gloves my daddy bought me!" Gia's always been a daddy's girl—big time. "I just know he's going to get me a new car for Christmas. I love him so much!"

"Tell me about it," Rachel replies sarcastically.

"I'm sorry," Gia replies. "I forgot that you don't... have a dad."

Rachel laughs. "Everyone has a dad, Gia. I just have no idea who mine is!"

"Does it bother you?" Gia asks with genuine concern.

Rachel shrugs.

"Not really. Before my mom left, it kind of felt like it was the two of us against the world. I never felt like I needed a dad. I was happy."

"Did your mom ever tell you about him?"

Rachel sighs. "My mom said my dad was a Peace Corps volunteer who died from dysentery in Africa."

"What about his extended family?" Gia asks.

"My mom said he didn't have any other family."

"And you believe her?"

"At the time I did," Rachel admits. "It seems pretty silly now, though. But she said something the night she disappeared. She said she'd tell me the truth—about everything."

"I'm so sorry, Rachel," Gia consoles. "Does it still bother you, not knowing?"

"Like I said before, I never felt like I needed a dad... I just want my mom back."

The friends continue driving to the mall in silence.

Chapter Nine

~~CRISSY DOBSON~~ AND ~~BLAKE BALQUIST~~

Back on Spalding Avenue, Crissy Dobson and Blake Balquist are about to get busy.

They were high school sweethearts before heading off to separate colleges last Fall. Long distance relationships are tough, but reunions are sweet. The couple plans on spending as much time together as possible during their winter break.

Crissy runs down the hallway screaming with girlish glee. She turns into her bedroom and hops onto her bed. She's wearing sexy red velvet lingerie lined with faux white fur.

Blake, equally excited, comes crashing in after her. He's wearing a silk Santa hat with matching red boxers. He smiles lustfully at Crissy.

"Close your eyes and open your mouth," he coaxes. "I got a big package ready for delivery!"

Crissy giggles joyfully as Blake charges at her and jumps on the bed. He grabs her and smothers her with kisses. She wraps her legs around his waist.

He pulls back.

"When did you say your parents are coming back?"

"I told you," Crissy chides. "They went to the cabin for the weekend. I'm all yours, Loverboy!"

Blake moves back in for more smooching, but Crissy evades him and slides off the bed. She walks over to her dresser and opens a drawer, looking back at Blake seductively.

Blake raises his eyebrows.

"What you got going on over there?" he asks.

"I went snooping through my parents' room, and..." She doesn't finish her sentence. Instead, she pulls objects out of the drawer and sets them on top of the dresser: toys, whips, feathers, clamps, and a set of furry handcuffs.

Crissy picks up a whip and gives it a crack.

Blake watches in awe. He's impressed.

"Damn, girl! What have they been teaching you at college?" He leans over the nightstand and turns on the radio. Shade's "Sweetest Taboo" is playing. Erotic energy surges.

Crissy begins to sway and dance; she's a bit clumsy, but her confidence is sexy. She hops up on the dresser and kicks a leg in the air, inadvertently knocking over a lamp. It shatters across the floor.

"Don't stop dancing," Blake says. "Blame it on the maid!"

Crissy climbs down from the dresser, gathers her treasures, and slinks back towards Blake like Catwoman.

"Do you feel adventurous?" she asks.

"I thought having sex while your parents were out *was* adventurous."

She giggles, dropping her sexy cache on the nightstand. She picks out four leather straps with buckles and hold them up for Blake to see.

"What are those for?" he asks.

"Adventure," is her coy and sexy reply. Forceful and domineering, she quickly straps Blake's right ankle to a bed post.

"Hold up... what are you doing?"

"You're not scared, are you?" she teases, making pouty lips.

He's scared stiff—and he likes it! There's no way he can resist her. Crissy continues strapping Blakes appendages to her bed posts.

"What if there's an emergency?" He's quivering with nervous excitement.

"Pick a safe word," she advises. "If things get too wild for you to handle, you just say the safe word and I'll stop. I promise." She smiles while binding Blake's right wrist to the bed post with an extra tug.

"How 'bout... Jingle Balls!"

They both laugh as Crissy finishes wrapping the final strap around Blake's left wrist. She stands back, looking down at her conquest triumphantly. Blake is completely blown away.

"I would never have guessed that your parents were into this shit!"

"You look so helplessly cute." She licks her lips. "I'll be right back with a big surprise."

"Where are you going?" Blake asks, his voice cracking just a bit.

"Kitchen!" she replies with a wink.

"Hurry back, okay?" he calls after her. "Okay?"

She doesn't reply. The kitchen's bathed in colorful pools of light emanating from a string of blinking orbs framing the window. She notices something on the counter: a pair of rusty metal garden shears.

But she's got other things on her mind.

Crissy opens the refrigerator and begins gathering supplies: a canister of whipped cream, a basket of strawberries, a jar of peanut butter. She places them on the counter next to the shears and goes back for more: chocolate syrup, baby carrots, and giant pickles. She turns around to place them on the counter.

Suddenly, Killer Santa, who was waiting in the shadows, grabs the shears and drives the blades upward, through Crissy's chin, jaw, nasal cavity, and brain. The rusty ends of the blades pierce her skull cap. Blood gurgles from the penetration points, splashing on the counter, creating slick puddles the floor.

She never even saw it coming.

Beautiful, the evil mask hisses.

"Babe?" Blake calls from the bedroom. "I'm pretty horny over here!"

He freezes when he sees a familiar figure in the doorway. Red and white suit, pointed cap, long white beard.

"Now that's kinky!" Blake shakes his head and laughs. "Your parents are sick as fuck!"

There's no reply.

"Babe?" His smile fades. He looks at his limbs, each securely bound to a bedpost. He panics. "To be honest. I've never been interested in fucking Santa."

Look at that bulge in his boxers, the mask says to its owner. *He doesn't deserve it! That should be yours!*

The maniac moves from the doorway and creeps towards the helpless boy.

"How about I wear the Santa costume?" Blake says. "I'm tired of you always getting to be on top!"

The lurching horror stands over him, looking down.

"What's that you got behind your back..." he whines. "Babe?"

The monster swings the rusty blades around.

"Jingle Balls! Jingle Balls! Jingle Ba-"

JOSEPH A. MILLIGAN

Chapter Ten

WHO TOOK THE MERRY OUT OF CHRISTMAS?

After parking the car, Rachel and Gia walk towards the mall, passing a colorful Christmas tree lot.

"Are you crazy?" Gia yells. "There's no way I'm spending my Saturday night decorating that woman's house."

"Please!" Rachel persists. "Mrs. Garrett's actually a very sweet woman. It'll be fun. I promise."

"Don't you remember how that house scared the shit out of us when we were kids?" Gia remembers throwing rocks at the house and making faces at the girl in the window when she was younger. At night, however, she stayed as far away from that eerie place as possible.

"That was just kids telling ghost stories," Rachel persists. "She's just lonely and trying to get back into the world. How would you feel if your husband went to jail and your child disappeared?"

"I'd feel free." Gia does a little twirl to illustrate her sentiment. A husband and kids sound like imprisonment to her. She dreams of traveling to Europe and South America, having creative polyamorous adventures all along the way.

"It's easy for you to joke about because you've never lost anyone in your family," Rachel says.

Oh Go, not another guilt trip, Gia thinks.

"I don't know," Gia says out loud. "I want to spend time with you, but that old lady always gave me the creeps."

"We don't have to go over until we're done shopping," Rachel continues. "Show a little Christmas spirt. I promise, once you meet her, you'll see how sweet she really is."

"Yeah, well... we'll see I guess."

"You're the best!" Rachel squeezes her friend's arm.

They arrive at an indoor shopping mall and head inside. They spot a massive Christmas Tree in the center court yard and run over to it like children. Gia takes out her phone and starts taking selfies.

Someone calls out to them.

"Rachel! Gia!"

It's Sarah Blair. Back in high school, they were like the Three Musketeers, thick as thieves, ride or die. Sarah's taller than her friends; athletic and good-looking with mischievous eyes. Rachel and Gia hurry towards her; they come together in a group hug.

"It's so good to see you, Rachel," Sarah coos. "You've been gone too long!"

"Thanks, Sarah," Rachel replies. "You look amazing—as always."

Sarah takes a step back and strikes a pose.

"What, this old thing?" She bats her eyelashes and makes duck-lips.

Rachel and Gia laugh. *Typical Sarah!*

"Guess what, Rachel!" Sarah sounds deliciously sinister. "I have a major surprise for you."

Rachel looks at Gia worried. Gia just shrugs her shoulders.

"I think you're scaring me," Rachel replies half-heartedly.

Sarah smiles as she grabs Rachel's hand, leading her away. Gia following close behind.

"Close your eyes, Rachel. No peeking!"

"Oh my God," Rachel replies. "Are we twelve-years-old again?"

Sarah giggles, pulling Rachel around a couple of corners and into the food court.

"Okay, stand here," Sarah advises. "Now... open your eyes!"

Rachel opens her eyes.

"Surprise!" Sarah yells.

Rachel's smile fades. She finds herself face to face with Cody Harris, her ex-boyfriend. Rachel broke up with him via text message the night she left for college. She knew she was breaking his heart and couldn't bear it. She blocked him on her phone, email, and all social media.

And now, all this time later, here he is: insecure and nervous, his face a mixture of anticipation and fear. He carries a somewhat nerdy charm. Rachel glances back at Sarah, giving her a death stare.

Sarah smiles.

Gia shrugs.

Cody pulls a single limp rose out from behind his back and holds it out for Rachel.

"Don't blame Sarah," he implores. "I put her up to it. It seemed like there wasn't any other way to get through to you. I had to do something." He pauses in order to let Rachel respond, but she's still angry and silent. "Merry Christmas."

Rachel looks at the rose and back up at Cody, speechless.

"We're gonna go take a lap around the mall," Sarah says, tugging Gina away.

Gia mouths the word "Sorry" as they retreat.

Sarah and Gia slink back into the crowded mayhem of the shopping mall, leaving the uncomfortable couple alone.

"Can we talk?" Cody asks.

Chapter Eleven

CHRISTMAS TIME'S A-COMING

Mrs. Garrett looks herself over in the full-length mirror on her bedroom door.

"Tonight's the night," she whispers to herself.

She's wearing her smartest Christmas outfit, a sweater and skirt combination. Her hair is up, impeccably coiffed and flawless. She applies a coat of bright red lipstick.

"Tonight," she whispers, "everything will be in its place again. Everything will be as it should have been—everything will be perfect."

When Rachel returns, Mrs. Garrett will tell her everything.

"Time to set the table."

She heads downstairs towards the dining room. She makes a detour to the basement in order to ensure that the recently installed padlock on the door is still secure. She gives the massive lock a couple of hard pulls. It's locked up tight. She smiles.

Her ears perk up. She thinks she hears something: creaking, someone in the shadows, or maybe just outside. Mrs. Garrett steels herself.

"Is that you?" she asks in a controlled tone, slowly heading into the living room. "The policeman said you might come to pay me a visit. But I told him you didn't have the *balls*. Get it?"

She laughs at her own private joke.

Chapter Twelve

ALL I WANT FOR CHRISTMAS IS YOU

Rachel bites the tip of a hotdog and chews. Cody squirms in his seat, uncomfortably.

"Is it good?" he asks.

Rachel can barely hear him over the din of the food court.

"It's okay," she replies, giving him an awkward thumbs-up.

Cody can't hold back. He's been waiting a year for this.

"What the hell happened to you?" He's trying to be calm, but his emotions betray him; his voice is shaking. "You could've at least mentioned that you were going off to college. I would have accepted a letter... or an E-mail... or a freakin' Post-It Note. You just blocked me and left."

This is exactly what Rachel hoped to avoid forever: bearing witness to the pain in Cody's eyes—the pain she caused him. But how could she have explained that he reminded her too much of things she was trying to forget without hurting him even more?

"I just didn't know how to tell you," she explains. "And it wasn't just you. I left everyone. Gia, Sarah, my grandma..."

"At least you called *them* when you came back to visit."

Touché, Cody.

Why are you so needy? she wonders. How could she explain

that her own emotional trauma was too great to shoulder anyone else's?

"There's so much I'm trying to resolve, Cody." It would be easier if she could just tell him to fuck off, but she can't. "I'm trying to move on with my life and I'm terrified of getting stuck... here."

She's is Cody's first true love. They lost their virginities to each other. They went to prom together. They were voted "Cutest Couple" by their classmates. He's clearly not ready to give up.

"Whatever it is, I'll help you."

"You can't, Cody," she tells him flatly. "You're not like me. You have a family. All I've got is my grandma. Once she passes away, the bank will repossess her house and I'll be alone. I'll have nothing."

Cody inhales deeply, overwhelmed by the depth of Rachel's misery.

"Do you think your mom's... still alive?"

"I hope so," Rachel replies, her emotions rising.

"What about your dad?" Cody suggests tentatively. "Maybe it's not too late to find him. What if you have a family out there... somewhere."

"My mom told me my father died in Africa," Rachel says, scratching her chin. "But my grandma would never confirm it. Maybe she knows more than she's willing to admit."

"You could ask her again," Cody suggests. "You're an adult now and you have a right to know."

Rachel nods slowly but says nothing

Cody places a hand on hers.

"Thanks for talking to me again," he says tenderly. "I missed this."

Rachel smiles wanly, but says nothing.

"Will you start taking my calls again?" Cody flashes big, sad, puppy dog eyes. "Please?"

Rachel can't fight it. "Okay. You win. I'll unblock you."

Sarah and Gia, seemingly waiting for their cue, suddenly approach.

"How's it going, lovebirds?" Sarah asks.

Rachel rises, grabs Sarah's arm, and pulls her aside.

"You're going to pay for this." Her voice is stern, her jaw is clenched.

"Take a chill pill, Rachel," Sarah replies. "I thought I was doing you a favor."

Rachel scoffs. "You want to do me a favor? Fine. I'll give you a chance to do me a *real* favor." She crosses her arms across her chest. "I hope you don't have plans tonight, Sarah."

Sarah's shit-eating smile fades.

Chapter Thirteen

MAKE EVERY DAY A HOLIDAY

Mrs. Garrett sits down in her dining room. The table is set for a special occasion with her best dinnerware, crystal wine glasses, and a lovely candelabra. She dips a spoon into a hearty bowl of Christmas stew and smiles.

She think she's alone, but she isn't. To her right sits an exceptionally handsome Santa Claus mannequin. To her left sits the pretty female mannequin wearing a dazzling sequin gown. Suddenly, Mrs. Garrett's smile grows cold.

She turns abruptly towards the handsome Santa.

"What did you say to me?" she grumbles, tossing her spoon aside.

Behind his own bowl of Christmas stew, the handsome Santa stares back at her with plastic eyes.

"Just once, I'd like to have a nice dinner without you picking a fight with me!" She flies into a rage. "You make me sick. Maybe next time, *you'll* make dinner and *I'll* say it tastes like hot shit! How would you like that?" Mrs. Garrett turns away, holding back tears. "You haven't even said anything about how I look tonight."

The handsome Santa does not reply.

Mrs. Garrett collects herself, wiping her tears with a cloth napkin. She sighs. She knows she shouldn't be too hard on him. She's been on quite a journey during her hermitage, and he's always been her constant—her Rock of Gibraltar.

Without him, why, she isn't even sure she'd want to be alive.

"Forgive me," she says, looking into the handsome Santa's soulless eyes. "Nothing will ruin this special night." She smiles. "Everything will be perfect—as soon as the guest of honor arrives."

Chapter Fourteen

A CREATURE WAS STIRRING

The wind picks up as Rachel, Gia, and Sarah, all on foot, approach the Creepy Christmas House on Spalding Road. Rachel's still incensed over Sarah's antics; the surprise reunion with her ex.

"That was so cringey!" Rachel yells at Sarah.

"So-rry," Sarah replies dismissively. "I didn't think you were gonna freak out."

"What did you expect to happen?"

"I don't know," Sarah says. "A little Christmas romance? A sexy holiday adventure? I thought you just needed a little push."

"I'd like to give you a little push," Rachel replies. "Right into a pool of piranhas!"

Gia nods in agreement.

Sarah rolls her eyes.

"Well, we're here," Rachel announces.

They pause in front of the mob of mannequin Santas.

"Jesus Christ," Sarah gasps. "This place is even creepier than I remember!"

"You owe me," Rachel reminds her. "Big time."

"Fine!" Sarah throws her hands in the air. "Let's get this over with."

They walk to the door and Rachel knocks.

"Behave yourselves!" She tells her friends.

The girls laugh, but go quiet when the door opens, revealing the infamous Mrs. Garrett, the witch of childhood horror stories. Her expression of joy fades when she realizes that Rachel is not alone.

"Hi, Mrs. Garrett," Rachel beams. "I hope you don't mind I brought my friends along to help. It isn't too late, is it?"

Gia and Sarah smile politely.

"Gia Remmy and Sarah Blair." Mrs. Garrett look each of them up and down. "I remember you both. Please, won't you come in out of the cold." She steps to the side and opens her arms, welcoming them.

The girls enter the house and look around. Sarah immediately notices a few stray Santa mannequins propped up against the walls in the living room. She mouths the word "Fuck!" Gia suppresses a giggle.

"Where do you want us to start, Mrs. Garrett?" Rachel asks.

"I'm so thankful for the help, girls!" Mrs. Garrett assures them. "But I forgot to tell you earlier that I have a date tonight. I shouldn't be gone for too long."

Sarah smiles and raises her eyebrows.

"Hot date?" she asks. "That's moving pretty fast for a woman who hasn't been out of the house in fifteen years."

"Then again," Sarah continues, "If I'd been holed-up for fifteen years, I'd be on the prowl for some BDE, you better believe it!"

Mrs. Garrett suppresses her ire and replies politely.

"I didn't say it was a romantic date. Heavens no. That part of my life died when my husband was taken away. I'm celibate and content to stay this way." Mrs. Garrett gestures for the young woman to proceed further inside. "Please do make your-selves at home."

Gia strolls into the living room; a chill runs up her spine as she approaches the haunting mannequins. The fireplace is lined with dozens of flameless candles. She picks one up.

Mrs. Garrett approaches her. "Flameless candles," she gushes. "Is there anything better?"

"Actually," Gia replies, "this is the first time I've ever seen one in person."

"I saw them advertised on TV late one night," Mrs. Garrett continues, "and I couldn't believe my eyes. It was absolutely amazing. I know they aren't real, but it's so fun to pretend. Sometimes I'll even try to blow them out! Can you just imag-ine?" She laughs out loud, an enthusiastic cackle, like she's just recounted the most interesting story ever told.

The girls listen politely, clearly thinking otherwise.

"So..." Rachel steers the conversation away from flameless candles. "Did you have a list of things you needed done, Mrs. Garrett?

"I do!" she replies enthusiastically. "Right this way!" She heads into the kitchen with the trio following close. There's a to-do list on the refrigerator.

"I mostly need some boxes brought down from the attic." She points at the list. "I also have more lights I'd like strung up outside. Oh, and I haven't decorated the bathrooms yet.

"There's plenty of food in the fridge," Mrs. Garrett says, as she gestures toward fresh cookies that are laid out on an adjacent counter, along with a glass pitcher of eggnog.. "And I would be deeply insulted if you didn't have a glass of my holiday eggnog before you go." She smiles extra wide—like a shark. "It's my specialty!"

"Okay, Mrs. Garrett," Rachel says. "We'll get started right away."

"One more thing before I leave," Mrs. Garrett looks down at

her watch, then back at Rachel. "Let me show you the attic where... I keep the extra decorations." Without giving her time to react, Mrs. Garrett takes Rachel's hand and leads her away.

Mrs. Garrett's hand are clammy, almost wet.

Sarah and Gia are left alone, creeped out and perturbed.

Unseen eyes watch them from behind a window.

Naughty, naughty! the black mask hisses.

Chapter Fifteen

HOLIDAY SPIRIT

Mrs. Garrett takes Rachel up the stairs and down a long, dim hallway. They pass an open doorway into a little girl's room. Rachel pauses, noticing a rag doll on the bed, bathed in eerie blue moonlight.

She steps inside.

Mrs. Garrett watches, making no objection.

The room is pretty pink perfection, like something straight off a showroom floor. There's a wall of old porcelain dolls sitting in rows on shelves. There's a table with a large round mirror, an ideal place for playing dress-up. The blankets and pillows on the bed are shades of cotton-candy and bubblegum. A painted sign on the headboard reads: *"Jamie's Room."*

Rachel's drawn to the rag doll; it seems to beckon her, like a voice from a dream. She picks it up as Mrs. Garrett continues observing her.

"Is this…" Rachel turns to face the old lady while taking a seat on the bed. "Is this the doll I brought for Jamie for Christmas one year?"

Mrs. Garrett takes a seat beside her.

"Jamie loved that doll."

The memory floods back: *young Rachel looking up into a window. Jamie's despondent face peers down at her, long clumps of black hair obscuring her face.*

"I remember... feeling sad and—wanting to be her friend."

Mrs. Garrett and Rachel lose themselves in thoughts.

"Can I ask you something, Mrs. Garrett?"

"Of course, dear."

"Why couldn't Jamie come out and play with the other kids? It looked like she wanted to join us, the way she always watched us from up here so intently."

Mrs. Garrett walks to the window and looks out, dazed.

The children used to play games at the edge of the forest, building forts, and making joyful noises. That was back before the woods got a reputation for being haunted.

Mrs. Garrett is lost in reverie.

"She was just too fragile," Mrs. Garrett explains as though she's looking at a ghost. "She needed me to protect her."

The room fills with sadness, regret, and terrible loneliness. Rachel's heavily burdened heart breaks just a little bit more. "You did what you thought was best," she says.

Mrs. Garrett smiles. "I most certainly did."

"They don't want to play with you, baby," Mrs. Garrett assures Jamie. "They're selfish. and spoiled rotten." She'll say whatever it takes to convince the child. "They don't have a good mama like you do," she lies.

Then, like an unspoken contradiction, there she is: young Rachel, standing outside, looking up at the window.

"Those children won't understand you," Mrs. Garrett tells Jamie, growing frustrated. "They'll make fun of you because you're different."

Like an antidote to venom, young Rachel holds a rag doll up for Jamie to see. It infuriates Mrs. Garrett.

"They're awful, awful people." Her voice trembles.

There's a tag around the rag doll's neck: "To Jamie. Merry Christmas!"

"Come away from the window," she commands Jamie. "Don't torture yourself like this!"

Jamie doesn't move.

Mrs. Garrett fights to control her emotions.

"This whole neighborhood is going straight to hell!" She screams with enough force to startle young Rachel who scurries back home, dropping the rag doll.

Mrs. Garrett glares out the window, watching young Rachel run.

"Naughty, naughty..."

"What's that Mrs. Garrett?" Rachel asks.

Mrs. Garrett snaps back to the here-and-now.

"Nothing, dear." She returns to the bed and sits beside Rachel.

"I always believe that positive reinforcement is very important for a child's mental health," she states without a shred of self-awareness.

"Thank you for opening up to me about Jamie," Rachel replies. "I always wondered why you and Jamie were so isolated from everyone." She takes a nervous breath. "I hope you don't mind my asking, but... what happened to Jamie?" She can sense Mrs. Garrett tensing up. "It's just that there are so many awful rumors. Is she still alive?"

"When the time is right, I'll tell you everything. I promise."

Chapter Sixteen

KRAMPUS

"**W**hat the fuck is taking them so long?" Sarah complains.

She and Gia are downstairs in the Garrett House, waiting for Rachel and the strange lady to return from the attic.

Gia's looking at a wall covered with colorful Christmas cards in the vestibule. "It looks like Mrs. Garrett hasn't gotten a new Christmas card in, like, fifteen years," she notes.

"Why are we here?" Sarah asks. "We always thought this woman was nuts."

"I don't know," Gia replies. "You know Rachel. She has a soft heart. She feels sorry for her... I guess."

"I knew something like this was bound to happen," Sarah says. "This is exactly why I tried to set her up with Cody: so we wouldn't get roped into one of her crazy plans."

"Sarah!" Gia gasps.

"I'm just saying what we're both thinking," Sarah shoots back.

They hush up as Rachel and Mrs. Garrett descend the staircase.

Mrs. Garrett's carrying Jamie's rag doll.

"Well, I'm off. Now, don't you girls do anything too dangerous," she warns the trio ominously. "Safety first. There's a flashlight on the table for the attic." She sets the doll down at the bottom of the stairs before donning her jacket and a warm scarf. She puts her purse over her shoulder and smiles.

"Have a wonderful time, Mrs. Garrett," Rachel says. "You deserve it."

Mrs. Garrett stares at the girls in silence for a moment. "I just can't believe this," she says. "I remember seeing the three of you playing in the streets. Now, just look at you..."

The girls smile back awkwardly as Mrs. Garrett exits through the front door.

"Thank you for your help," Mrs. Garrett concludes, shutting the door behind her.

For a moment, the crackling of the fire is the only sound in the house.

Sarah breaks the silence. "Who would've thunk?" she asks, putting her hands on her hips. "Mrs. Garrett's a whore."

They're finally free to laugh their asses off.

"At least someone's getting their kicks tonight," Gia joshes.

The girls look out the living room window. They watch Mrs. Garrett get into her car and drive away.

Sarah plops down in a fluffy chair and props her legs up, grabbing a nearby magazine.

"Well, I'm sure you ladies can take it from here," she says with nonchalance. "I'm just going to sit back, relax, and read..." she looks at the cover and cringes, "...*The Quilting World*?"

"Hey, look at this." Gia points at the windowsill. "The window's been screwed shut. Why would anyone do that?"

Rachel walks next to Gia and examines the window herself. Sure enough, Gia was right.

"Maybe she's really concerned about people trying to get in?" Rachel hypothesizes.

"Locks keep people from getting in," Gia says. "Screws keep people from getting out."

An uncomfortable silence falls over them.

"I'm sure it's just for added security," Rachel says after a moment. "I mean, she *does* live alone."

Sarah motions at all the mannequins. "That's debatable."

"I have to admit," Gia puts her arms around herself as though suppressing a shiver, "the mannequins are creeping me out. This whole place is creeping me out."

"I say we blow this joint," Sarah says while tossing the magazine aside and standing up.

"Oh, come on you guys," Rachel says. "We can't just bail on her now."

"It's not just the screwed up windows, mannequins and flameless candles that are strange, Rachel," Gia says. "Come here. I want to show you something else." She walks over to the Christmas tree and points at the dozen-or-so presents beneath it. "All of these presents are addressed to Jamie."

"What?" Rachel gets on her knees to investigate the presents for herself.

"Can you believe this?" Gia asks. "No one in their right mind would do something like this, right?"

"Well, I don't know... maybe it just makes her feel better."

Sarah scoffs. "Maybe she's just cuckoo for Cocoa Puffs?"

Rachel gets defensive. "Is it wrong for her to hold on to the hope that Jamie will come back someday?"

"Come back?" Gia replies. "I thought she was killed?"

"There have been so many crazy rumors over the years," Rachel says. "Mrs. Garrett's the only one who really knows what happened."

"I know what happened," Sarah says, hovering over them.

Rachel and Gia look back at her, shocked. "Bullshit," they say in unison.

"It's true." Sarah sits back down on the sofa to tell her tale.

"I was in Kindergarten, and Jonathan Curtis, who used to live down this very street, told me she was snatched right out of her bed in the middle of the night."

"We've all heard that rumor," Rachel replies. "That she was kidnapped."

"Yeah," Sarah retorts, "but that's not all Jonathan told me. He told me *who* snatched Jamie away."

Rachel and Gia's eyes grow wide.

"Who?" they ask.

"She was taken by some hideously deformed creature called... Krampus! Grr!" Sarah gnashes her teeth and makes finger claws. She howls.

"What the hell's a Krampus?" Gia asks.

Rachel rolls her eyes. "Don't listen to her, Gia. Krampus is just an urban legend."

"That's what you think," Sarah says. "Krampus is the exact opposite of Santa Claus. He kidnaps and tortures children who misbehave during the Christmas season. In fact," she pauses for dramatic effect, "...Krampus could be here now—lurking in the shadows!"

At that very moment, an off-kilter Santa mannequin slides off a wall, noisily falling to the floor.

The girls scream. When they realize what happened, they laugh.

"You're so stupid," Rachel tells Sarah, still clutching her sides. "I can't believe you ever took Jonathan seriously!"

"Hey, I was only five-fucking-years-old," Sarah says, "and Jonathan scared the shit out of me with that story. I had nightmares for years. I would always dream that I was trapped out in the woods and Krampus was chasing me. I could see my home, but he would always appear and chase me away... further into the woods." Sarah sours for a moment. "Come to think of it, Jonathan Curtis destroyed my childhood!"

"Ironic how you lost your virginity to him in high school," Gia jabs.

"I know, right?" Sarah replies. "I guess he destroyed my childhood *and* my adolescence."

Rachel sees a new porcelain doll under the Christmas tree.

"What are you thinking about?" Gia asks.

"Mrs. Garrett has told me some stuff about Jamie."

"What did she say?" Sarah asks.

"She said Jamie had something called Bowen's Disease," Rachel says. "But I don't think Mrs. Garrett ever told her. She just kept her isolated out of a sense of fear. Poor Jamie... wherever she is."

Chapter Seventeen

<del>MANDY CARPENTER</del> AND <del>BETH MERRIN</del>

Further down Spalding Road, Mandy Carpenter is getting ready for a night of non-denominational holiday frolicking with her girlfriend Beth Merrin. Her room is decked out in flashing purple lights and candles. A stick of incense sends threads of white smoke towards the ceiling. The bed's dressed in silk sheets.

Mandy's wearing a classic teddy beneath her long silk robe. She looks herself over in the mirror, and smiles. She sticks her head out the door of her room and calls down the hall towards the bathroom.

"You're in for a treat tonight!"

No response; just the sound of streaming water from the shower.

Mandy shivers, noticing the window's been left wide open.

Jesus Christ, babe! she thinks. *Are you trying to freeze me to death?* She walks to the window and looks at the front yard before closing it. She pulls the curtains closed as well. The chill in the air subsides as Mandy disrobes and gets into bed.

"I hope you're feeling frisky!" she calls down the hall.

No response; just the sound of running water.

Mandy notices a book on her nightstand. She loves books.

"Don't take too long," she calls down the hall. "If I start reading, you know there's no stopping me."

Mandy would put everything on hold for a good book, even going so far as to call in sick from work one time in order to read.

"Last chance, babe," she calls down the hall. "Speak now or forever hold your *piece*!" She giggles despite knowing that her pun will be lost. "Humph!" She grabs the book. "Your loss!"

She dives in, quickly losing herself in a world of pulpy, soapy, incestuous horror.

She's reading *Butcher, Baker, Nightmare Maker* by Joseph Burgo. It's the book that inspired the movie of the same name, directed by William Asher and released in 1981. She saw the movie in her teens and absolutely loved the madcap absurdity of it all.

Susan Tyrrell (who starred as Cheryl Roberts) is, in Mandy's opinion, one of cinema's true artists, an unsung master, a female equivalent to Jack Nicholson. Mandy sought out all of her films and devoured them. She absolutely adored her as Queen Doris in *Forbidden Zone* (directed by Richard Elfman and first released in 1980); she even read the novelization by Joshua Millican.

But the *Butcher, Baker, Nightmare Maker* novelization is her favorite book. She loves the book more than the movie, of course. Burgo's novel is filled with detailed character descriptions, backstories, and a plot-line that continues well past the movie's ending.

She found her copy at a used bookstore in Berkeley a few years ago. The pages are worn at the corners, soft and comforting like warm skin.

The bed rocks, once, startling Mandy out of her book.

"What the?" She can still hear the shower running in the bathroom down the hall.

The bed rocks once again, as if someone, or something, is squirming underneath it.

Mandy's eyes bulge as she processes the implications of her situation. Her pulse quickens as she bolts up, steadying herself on her knees and fingertips.

The bed rocks once again.

She wants to run, but can't shake the image of someone reaching out to grab her the second her feet hit the floor. It's almost paralyzing. Instead, she cranes her neck slowly over the edge of the bed, investigating with trepidation. Her breathing quickens.

Without warning, rusty blades pierce the center of the mattress; they split the sheets mere inches from Mandy's right hand. As quickly as they came, the blades disappear again.

Mandy jolts back against the headboard and screams.

"Babe!"

Nothing from down the hall; just the sound of running water still.

The rusty blades emerge with another sinister rip—right between her legs, nearly nicking her most intimate folds.

She scrambles back on her hands and knees as the rusty blades finally connect, skewering her left palm. Mandy shrieks in agony and begins hyperventilating. Her fight or flight reflexes ignite; she springs from the mattress, gushing blood.

A hand reaches out and grabs her around the ankle before her foot even hits the ground.

Mandy falls flat on her face, fracturing her occipital bone. She turns and sees sick, burning eyes staring at her—eyes that seemed to be floating in an infinite void. She screams again, struggling for her life.

Kill her now! the hideous mask hisses. *Tear her open!*

The stalking, killer Santa pulls Mandy under the bed with him. She's engulfed in a cacophony of violent evisceration. Her blood creates a massive puddle, like melted wax, like a crimson lake.

Down the hall, the rushing shower spray finally ceases.

Beth Merrin turns the faucet off and swipes excess water off of her body. She removes a couple of waterproof earbuds and sets them in a soap dish. She opens the shower curtain and reaches for a towel.

Beth steps out of the shower and stands before the mirror, drying herself. She admires her reflection, specifically her biceps and her new tattoos. She calls out to Mandy:

"I hope you're feeling frisky, babe!"

No response.

"Babe? Did you hear me?" Beth tosses her towel aside and opens a drawer, retrieving a pink strap-on. She steps gingerly through the leg loops and pulls the apparatus up around her waist, positioning it perfectly.

"Ready or not, here I come!" She swings open the door. Through a haze of steam and flashing purple lights, she sees him: the merry mutilator—his rusty garden shears dripping blood!

Beth freezes.

Now kill him! the evil mask commands. *Wait... what?*

Santa tilts his head to the side, confused by the silicon schlong between Beth's legs.

Beth slams the door shut and locks it, beyond terrified. She braces her back against it as an inhuman howl fills the house. She hears glass breaking, furniture shredding, and walls being demolished. Then silence.

Suddenly, rusty blades blast through the door, through Beth's spine and torso, emerging below her sternum like a baby alien. Her stomach explodes; blood gushes from her mouth, down her neck.

Santa breaks the door open with Beth still stuck to it, hanging in place.

Might as well take it, the mask advises.

He reaches around and snatches Beth's dildo... for his collection.

Chapter Eighteen

TOYS IN THE ATTIC

"**D**on't tell me you've never had a strange collection before?" Rachel's sifting through tubs of lights and ornaments.

"Nothing as strange as a house full of creepy Santas, Rachel," Gia replies, eying another row of red and white, bearded mannequins.

Sarah stokes the fireplace with an iron poker, stirring it for all the light and heat they can get.

"Collections are just a waste of time and money," she declares as though it's a matter of fact. "Only boring people who have nothing else to do collect things."

"Really?" Gia replies. "What about your collection of STDs?" She and Rachel have a good laugh at Sarah's expense.

Sarah shrugs it off like she always does. "Look. If I'm going to survive this night, I'm going to need something better to sip on than the old lady's eggnog."

"You could run down to the Shop and Stop," Rachel suggests. "They're open until midnight."

Sarah likes that idea. She snatches up her purse.

67

"Back in a flash, bitches." She flashes a peace sign on her way out the door.

Gia wanders into the dining room as Rachel continues sorting Mrs. Garrett's Christmas junk. She's drawn to the female mannequin in the glittering dress. She strokes the fabric, enchanted and mesmerized.

"Hey, Rachel," she calls. "You gotta see this."

Rachel joins Gia in the dining room.

"Whoa." The lone female mannequin in a house of bearded men makes her sad.

"I gotta try this dress on and take a picture," Gia says. "It's beautiful."

"I don't think it's a good idea," Rachel replies.

"Well, I think it's a *great* idea," Gia says. "This is going on Insta."

Rachel moans.

"I thought you wanted to hurry up and get this over with." She puts her hands on her hips. "We'll never finish if you and Sarah keep goofing around."

"It'll take one second. I swear!"

Rachel rolls her eyes.

"Just make it fast. I'm going to get the other boxes down from the attic."

Rachel notices the rag doll at the foot of the stairs. She feels compelled to put it back where she found it before proceeding to the attic. She makes a detour to Jamie's room and puts it on the bed, in its proper place.

She turns to exit but notices a thin piece of green plastic sticking out from under Jamie's mattress. She pulls it out: a small plastic T-Rex. She lifts the mattress and sees more toys hidden in the box-springs: Army men, Hot Wheels, baseball cards, and comic books.

"Okay..." she says out loud, to no one, before leaving and heading to the attic.

The attic is so cold Rachel can see her breath. She scans the cobwebbed realm with her flashlight, making a mental catalog of boxes, toys, and tubs of Christmas supplies. She sets the light down before crawling forward on her hands and knees.

Beside a red tub, Rachel spies an old box containing baby clothes and fading photographs. She's struck with curiosity and starts investigating. She opens a dusty photo album, and finds a picture of Jamie when she must have been around five-years-old.

The child's deep-set eyes are sad and full of resentment.

She rifles some more and finds a snapshot of Jamie, back turned, looking out the window.

She was probably watching us all play, Rachel thinks.

"You must have hated us," she whispers. "I'm so sorry, Jamie," she tells the picture.

Rachel flips the page, and the next photo show an old eight-by-ten black & white of a group of nurses. She examines the fading faces staring back at her, and she shivers, swallowing hard.

Confusion on her face, she puts her finger on one of the nurses in the photo.

"Mom?"

Chapter Nineteen

JONATHAN CURTIS

Sarah can't believe her eyes.

As fate would have it, Jonathan Curtis is working the counter at the Shop and Stop. There he is: the scourge of her childhood, the breaker of her hymen, standing between the cash register and display case of beef jerky.

"This is so weird," Sarah says, sauntering up to the counter with her wine of choice.

"Well, hello, Sexy Sarah!" He hasn't set eyes on her since he dropped out in 10th grade to form a nu-metal band called Jesus Crack. They toured the Bay Area for a while, until their drummer, Eddie Figarino, was electrocuted mid-show at a club in Pacifica.

"My friends and I were just talking about you," Sarah says, setting the bottle of wine down on the counter.

"Oh, yeah?" He's flattered. "Good stuff, I hope." He looks exactly the way Rachel remembers him, only his dreadlocks are longer and he has *way* more tattoos—even a tiny skull & crossbones on his face, between his sideburn and his right eye. He may be stuck working a dead-end job for minimum wage, but he still carries himself like a rockstar.

Damn. Boys who know they're good-looking are the worst! Sarah thinks.

"We were talking about Jamie Garrett," she explains. "I told them all about Krampus."

"Oh, God!" Jonathan shakes his head. "I haven't thought about that creepy little moppet in years. Remember when I threw poop at her window?"

"Yeah," Sarah looks disgusted. "It wasn't one of your brightest moments."

"What? It wasn't *my* poop," he says, as though that somehow makes his youthful prank less revolting.

"Yeah, well, you wouldn't believe where I'm hanging out tonight-"

"Damn, you still looking fine!" Jonathan interrupts. He looks her up and down while ringing her up and bagging her bottle. "You want to hang out for a little bit?" he asks, bobbing his eyebrows. "I could close-up for a while."

"You'd like that, huh?" Sarah teases.

"Yeah, I would!"

Sarah leans forward and snatches the bottle.

"No way!" She's not interested in treading down familiar paths. It's been a long time since she's messed with anyone as immature as Jonathan Curtis. "Have a nice night," she says in the sexiest voice she can summon.

Jonathan watches her ass swish out the door. Overcome with lust, he snatches up one of the errant porno magazines he keeps stashed under the counter (night shifts can get lonely, after all). He flips through it until he finds someone who vaguely resembles Sarah: a bleach-bottle blonde with a *Baywatch* bod and a bubble butt.

Usually, he takes care of this kind of business in a bathroom stall, but tonight he's on fire. He can't wait. He unfastens his belt and drops his trousers.

"Oh, yeah! Sexy Sarah!"

He doesn't see the hulking Santa standing outside, watching. *Another prick for the collection!* the evil mask hisses.

Chapter Twenty

IF I GET HOME ON CHRISTMAS DAY

The female mannequin in Mrs. Garrett's dining room is naked, and Gia looks amazing in its red sequin dress. She stands in front of a mirror, striking poses.

Mrs. Garrett may be a Grade-A old maid, but this dress is fly.

"Damn," Gia says out loud. "I look *good*!"

Rachel comes tearing downstairs, scaring the shit out of her.

"Look at this!" Rachel screams.

"Jesus Christ!" Gia replies, clutching her chest. "Give a girl a heart attack, why don't you!"

"Look!" Rachel shoves the old picture in Gia's face.

"So what," Gia replies. "Mrs. Garrett used to be a nurse." She turns back to her reflection. "How do I look? Are you ready to take some pictures of me?"

"Would you forget about that for a second," Rachel says. "I'm serious."

"Okay, fine." Gia takes the photo from her friend. "What am I looking at?"

"Look at the name of the person standing *next* to Mrs. Garrett," Rachel insists.

Gia looks at the face, then down at the list of names below the picture.

"Next to Vivian Garrett is... Laura Kimmell?" Gia gasps. "Oh my God!"

"That's my mother!" Rachel's nearly beside herself. "I'm freaking out!"

Gia freezes, shocked. "Are you fucking with me?"

"No!" Rachel says. "Mrs. Garrett lied to me!"

"What are you talking about?" Gia asks.

"We had a conversation earlier today," Rachel explains. "She said that she didn't know my mother—but she *had* to. They're standing right next to each other in this picture, for God's sake!"

"Why do you think she lied?" Gia asks.

Rachel can't even fathom the possibilities

"I have no idea..."

"What would she be hiding?" Another million-dollar question from Gia.

"This is insane!" Rachel declares, reaching for her cell phone. "If my mom and Mrs. Garrett knew each other, were maybe even friends, then my grandma *must* know more than she's saying."

"You really think so?"

Rachel nods. "That's the one thing I *am* certain of," she says as she dials Abbey's number. "No more secrets!"

Chapter Twenty-One

SILENT NIGHT

Abbey's relieved to see Rachel's car in the driveway when she arrives home from her bridge tournament. She wheels up the front porch, unlocks the door, and goes inside.

"Rachel?" she calls out. "Are you home, sweetheart?"

No response; except for Abbey, the house is empty.

She takes off her scarf and jacket, wheels into the living room, and reignites the fireplace. Soon, the room's bathed in a soothing amber glow. Abbey watches the flames for a while, losing herself in thought.

Poor Rachel, she thinks. Growing up without her mother couldn't have been easy, Abbey knows this. She did the best she could after Laura went missing; she tried to give her grand-daughter the life she deserved.

Had she succeeded?

Abbey sighs; her heart is heavy.

Was I too hard on her? she wonders. No, everything she'd done was for Rachel's protection. She was just a child—there's no way she would have ever understood.

She rolls over to the window and looks up and down the

quiet street; her gaze settles on the Garrett house and its legion of Santa Claus mannequins.

"Mrs. Garrett," Abbey grumbles. "What the fuck are you up to?"

She hopes, almost prays, that Rachel isn't gullible or soft-hearted enough to actually offer her assistance to the old coot. Who asks a neighbor who they hardly even know to decorate their house? *Weird!*

She doesn't see Mrs. Garrett's car in the driveway and hopes that means the house is empty. The thought of Rachel inside makes her nervous. The thought of Mrs. Garrett filling her granddaughter's head with ridiculous nonsense infuriates her.

Rachel's been through enough already! Behind every harsh decision Abbey has made, every seemingly closed-minded stance she took, every lie she told, was the desire to protect her grand-daughter. As a teenager, she'd walked towards the edge of despair. Would the truth, in Rachel's case, pull her away from the abyss, or send her tumbling into its depths?

Abbey wouldn't risk it. Rachel is all she has left in the world —even if, by necessity, she chose to live far away.

Abbey wheels over to the liquor cabinet and pours herself a triple whisky. She tosses it back; the amber liquid burns going down her esophagus and warms her core. She gasps and shakes her head.

If Rachel knew the truth, she thinks, *I might lose her forever*. Abbey won't allow that to happen.

She wheels down the hall and opens a closet door. She grabs an old cane and uses it to knock a shoe box off the top self. The box lands in her lap.

Abbey wheels back to the fireplace and begins examining its contents. Old letters, mostly; some pictures—and Rachel's birth certificate. Her father's name is right there in black and white.

It's scandalous!

She tosses the document into the fire. If Rachel never learns the truth, that's fine by her. Abbey downs the rest of her whisky before sifting through the box again.

Love letters, dozens of them: all addressed to her daughter Laura. They're filled with unfounded declarations and unkept promises. They're all signed, *"Forever Your Love—PG."*

Abbey heaps them all into the fireplace. They ignite with a powerful whoosh, as though doused with gasoline (or imbued with evil). A few burning bits of paper try to escape, but Abbey rounds them up, ensuring everything burns down to ash.

She looks at her watch, annoyed.

"Where the devil are you, Rachel?"

She goes to the bar and pours herself another triple whiskey. She wheels over to an old record player and starts a disc spinning. "It Came Upon a Midnight Clear" begins to play. Abbey returns to the fireside, growing glassy-eyed and dazed.

The phone rings, startling Abbey from her whiskey-induced stupor. She shakes her head a bit before wheeling over to pick up the receiver.

"Hello?"

It's Rachel, thank God.

"Grandma?" she sounds stern and emotional. "I need to ask you something. And please, be honest with me."

Abbey had become so accustomed to lying to Rachel over the years it was a reflex. "Sure, honey," she tells her granddaughter. "Come home and we'll discuss whatever's on your mind." Not likely.

"I need to know *now*, Grandma," Rachel insists. "Did you know that my mom and Mrs. Garrett used to work together? Do you know if they were friends?"

Abbey feels like she's in an airplane that has just lost cabin pressure.

"Where are you? What's that crazy witch told you?"

"Just tell me!" Rachel says.

No way, Abbey thinks. *Not like this. Not after everything I've done to protect you!*

"Don't tell me you're at that woman's house!" Abbey yells, nearly losing all control.

"Did you know that Mrs. Garrett knew my mother?" Rachel replies, her ire and frustration rising.

"Come home now!" Abbey commands.

"If you don't tell me right now," Rachel says, "I'll never go back to your fucking house again for the rest of my life!"

Abbey sighs. She hasn't cried in fifteen years, and she isn't going to start now. She swallows hard and replies.

"Yes, I knew."

"Where are you?" Abbey asks, her tone softening.

The phone disconnects.

"Rachel?" Abbey says. "Rachel? Are you still there?"

Chapter Twenty-Two

FATHER CHRISTMAS

Rachel pockets her cell phone down. Her mind's racing with confusion and speculation.

Gia comes to her side, offering comfort.

"Are you... okay?"

"No, I'm not okay," Rachel replies nearly weeping. "She knew! My grandma fucking knew! What else does she know that she's hidden from me? She's a liar—and so is Mrs. Garrett!"

Rachel heads to the kitchen for a glass of water.

Gia follows her in.

"And the worst part is," Rachel sighs, "my grandma let me think that I was crazy. That's called gaslighting, right?"

"I'm so sorry Rachel," Gia says gently.

"Don't worry about me," Rachel replies sarcastically. "I'm just doing what I always do around Christmas time. I'm emotional, right? I'm paranoid, right? I just need to let things go and move on with my life, right?" She gets a glass of water from the sink.

"Please, Rachel," Gia holds her friend by the shoulders. "Just calm down and we can talk this out."

Rachel's eyes are distant and pensive.

Gia chooses her words carefully.

"Have you ever considered that there might be... a reason your grandmother didn't want to tell you the truth?"

Rachel doesn't seem to hear the question, still sporting her thousand-yard stare. "I was certain my mom was going to be home on Christmas—because she *told* me."

"How did you feel when she didn't?" Gia asks. "Be honest with your emotions."

"I just shrugged it off. I told myself, she'll be here next year. The alternative was too horrible to face. And it never got easier like everyone said it would. As I got older, I felt worse... cheated. The craziest part is, I still can't shake this feeling that she's coming back. Right now, in fact, right here—I feel closer to my mother than ever!"

"Then let's find those answers," Gia says. "Let's tear this fucking house apart if we have to!"

"You'll really do that for me?" Rachel says, grateful.

"Ride or die," Gia assures her. "But can we at least get drunk afterwards?"

Rachel smiles and they hug, resolved.

"Let's get to work!"

They split up.

Gia remains downstairs as Rachel mounts the stairs. She heads straight to the end of the hallway and opens the door into Mrs. Garrett's room. She feels around in the dark for a light switch, and finds one.

There's a *click*.

She screams when she sees what looks like a body, covered by a sheet, in Mrs. Garrett's bed. She collects herself and moves slowly towards the bed, puzzled and incredulous. She pools her courage and pulls back the sheet.

She should have guessed.

Of course it's a Santa mannequin—and this one is sexy. His jacket is opened, his red pants around his thighs. He's smeared with red lipstick kisses on his face, chest, and groin. He looks sticky.

Relieved, she releases a blast of nervous laughter. But there's a hand on her shoulder! She screams again and spins around to see—Gia!

"What are you doing?" Rachel says.

"I heard you screaming!" Gia replies. "I came running up here to see if you were okay." She looks down at the bed and takes it all in, wrinkling her nose in disgust. "When you said Mrs. Garrett was lonely, you weren't kidding!"

The girls regard the sexy Santa together.

"What's her deal?" Gia asks. "Do you think she's mental?"

Rachel shakes her head.

"Maybe, they make her feel safe," Rachel says. She notices something on the nightstand. It's a framed picture of Mrs. Garrett and Mr. Garrett on their wedding day. She wasn't much older than Rachel and Gia are now.

"Whoa!" Gia looks over Rachel's shoulder at the picture. "Get a load of Mr. Garrett! How did a wack-job like her land a hunk like that!"

"Yeah, well," Rachel replies, "looks can be deceiving."

"I wonder if he ran off with a secret lover to start a new life?" Gia says. "That would be romantic."

"No, Gia," Rachel says. "He was a monster."

"What do you mean?"

"I met someone today who told me about him. A cop."

"A cop?" Gia replies. "What did he say?"

"He said Mr. Garrett used to abuse Mrs. Garrett and Jamie."

Gia is genuinely shocked. "No!"

"Yes!" Rachel insists. "It was so bad he was sent to the Readcrest Institute for the Criminally Insane!"

Gia gasps. "I've heard so many scary stories about that place!"

"That's not all," Rachel continues. "When the other inmates got ahold of him, they cut his dick off!"

"Shut up!"

"Yup!" Rachel starts putting puzzle pieces together in her mind. "In fact, I heard that cop saying something about a breakout." She scratches her chin. "I wonder of this has anything to do with Mrs. Garrett's mysterious date tonight?" Thoughts are racing, her heart is pounding. She turns to Gia. "Let's look for more clues!"

"Wait," Gia replies. "I found something downstairs that you're gonna want to look at."

"What is it?"

"A basement door—and it's locked."

Bingo. Rachel smiles. *No more secrets!*

"We need to find that key!"

Chapter Twenty-Three

BACK DOOR SANTA

Abbey's three sheets to the wind, drunk as a skunk, and completely shitfaced. She hasn't been this fucked up since her days riding with the Hell's Angels. They called her Abbey Stabbey back then. But that's another story.

She's looking at pictures of Rachel on the dining room table.

"I'm her grandmother!" Abbey screams at no one, a glass of whiskey sloshing in her right hand. "I know what's best for her! I decide what she should be told!" She yells toward the telephone, "Come on Rachel! Call me back! Come home!" She mumbles a litany of obscure obscenities.

Abbey hears a bump and a crash in the living room, like a vase getting knocked off an end table.

Startled, Abbey spills her whiskey on the old photos; the glass rolls of the table and across the hardwood floor.

"Rachel?" she calls out, slightly slurring.

She wheels her chair into the living room to investigate. Just as she suspected, her knock-off Ming vase is on the floor, shattered. The window above it is slightly ajar, the curtains billowing in the cold invasive wind.

Confounded, Abbey scans the room for anything else out of

place. She wheels herself slowly over to the window. The weather outside is growing frightful.

She peeks outside, tense as a rattlesnake.

A pitch-black cat yowls as it pounces inside, landing in Abbey's lap.

Abbey almost pees herself.

"Damn, Jasper!" she shouts. "You damn near ended me!"

Jasper meows.

"You want your kitty num-nums?" Abbey asks in a baby voice.

Jasper purrs.

Abbey closes the window, pivots her chair around, and wheels towards the kitchen. She passes the Christmas tree, adorned in lights and tinsel; an angel perched on top. She doesn't notice the shadowy figure hiding behind its branches; neither does Jasper.

Abbey grabs a bag of cat treats off the kitchen counter before proceeding out the back door and onto the porch. She's too drunk to feel the chill in the air. She feeds Jasper a few treats, scratches his chin, and strokes his back.

She looks up at the stars, then across her backyard, all the way into the steep ravine. It's about thirty yards of natural grass, with a vegetable garden along the fence (near a shed hiding a couple of cannabis plants). In happier days, the yard had been the site of barbecues, birthday parties, and casual keggers.

It's a beautiful view, even at night.

The door behind her creaks.

Jasper hisses, jumps away, and scampers off into the darkness.

Psychotic Santa, smoldering eyes floating in negative space, steps forward. Before Abbey can fully pivot around, he wraps duct-tape around her mouth, instantly muffling her screams.

Abbey tries to push the invader away, but he won't budge; he keeps her pinned to her chair.

He spins her, grabs the handles of her wheelchair—and pushes.

Abbey's face is wild with horror. She sees the edge of the ravine approaching. Her heart seizes.

Faster! the mask commands. *Make this old bitch fly!*

The murderer increases his speed, building momentum, grunting with every step.

The lip of the approaching ravine seems to open up, ready to devour her.

Abbey is launched into the darkness. She tumbles down across rocks, tree trunks, and into thorny branches. She crashes face-first into a boulder with a crunch, her wheelchair upending, its wheels spinning—going nowhere.

Killer Santa gazes down the cliff, shoulders heaving.

Excellent, coos the abominable mask.

Santa hears the phone ringing from inside the house and saunters back inside. He casually takes a seat in the living room. Jasper hops up into his lap, purring.

The answering machine clicks on.

"This is Abbey. Leave a message at the beep!"

The device beeps; a cassette tape whirrs.

"Grandma, it's Rachel."

The villain listens, petting Jasper sweetly.

"I'm sorry I hung up on you before. I'm still mad, but... I'm also worried about Mrs. Garrett. She left a little while ago, and I think her ex-husband might be coming for her. I think, maybe... all of this is connected. My mom, Mr. and Mrs. Garrett—maybe even Jamie..."

She'll know soon enough, the mask hisses.

Chapter Twenty-Four

AWAY IN THE MANGER

Rachel clutches her cell phone to her ear, pacing back and forth in Mrs. Garrett's kitchen.

"Grandma, please... pick up!"

No response.

"Call me when you get this. I love you, Grandma." Reluctantly, Rachel ends the call and pockets her cell phone again.

"Why wouldn't she answer?" Gia asks.

"She's probably drunk off her rocker," Rachel says. "I better go check on her." She heads to the door with Gia on her heels.

"Wait," Gia huffs. "Let me change out of this dress first."

"No," Rachel replies while putting on her jacket. "You better wait here."

Gia groans and slumps her shoulders.

"Sarah's going to be here any second," Rachel reminds her. "She'll freak out if we're both gone."

"Okay," she relents. "Just hurry, please!"

"I will," Rachel promises. "You keep looking for that key in the kitchen. Pour yourself a glass of eggnog while you're at it. I've got a feeling this is going to be a long night." With that, she rushes out the door, closing it behind her.

The wind whips Rachel's jacket and hair as she hurries down the quiet street towards her grandmother's home. She sees Abbey's van in the driveway.

She must be home, Rachel tells herself.

She gets to the porch and reaches into her pocket for keys. She hears slight movement inside—something hitting the floor.

"Grandma?" she calls while opening the door and stepping inside. She closes the door behind her and looks around. The house appears empty and quiet.

"Grandma... you here?" She scans the living room. She moves into the dining room, pausing briefly to look at the whiskey-soaked photographs on the table. Her apprehension rises. "Grandma?"

Rachel moves into the kitchen and gasps as Jasper runs past her and out the back door, which is wide open.

"Fucking cat!"

Jasper looks back at Rachel and meows.

The cat heads across the porch and into the backyard; Rachel follows, noticing the open door. Rachels walks into the backyard, and follows Jasper to the edge of the ravine.

She leans over the edge, saturated with dread.

"What the hell is going on tonight?"

Chapter Twenty-Five

SARAH ~~BLAIR~~

Sarah struts up Spalding Road clutching her bottle of cheap white wine. The street's deserted and quiet—unnervingly so. Her footsteps echo at an unnaturally hollow depth, as though she's descending a spiral staircase into oblivion.

It's cold, damp, and dreary, but Sarah's chipper, replaying her humiliation of Jonathan Curtis in her mind, smirking.

I bet that's the last time he acts so cocky! she thinks.

Sarah approaches the Creepy Christmas House, and pauses in front of the horde of mannequin Santas. She grunts in disgust.

"Crazy fucking loon," she gripes, shaking her head. "Creepy fucking Santas!"

There's a crash; a chain-link side-gate swings open.

Sarah jumps, collects herself, and creeps forward to investigate.

Without warning, a shopping cart full of dismembered mannequin limbs comes clamoring out. It wobbles, hits a bump, and spills its contents around Sarah's feet.

"Ha-ha, very funny!" she yells. "It's Christmas, not Halloween!"

No response; just the wind and crickets.

"Who's back there?" she asks. "I'll kick your ass, Gia!"

It isn't Gia.

Sarah sets the bottle down, brazenly making a beeline through the side yard. She follows a pathway, seeing a dark figure ahead.

"I'm gonna get you, Gia!"

The pathway veers into the woods. There's movement in the tree line.

"Gotcha!"

Sarah plunges into the trees. She stops a few yards in to let her eyes adjust to the darkness, straining to see the moon above the branches.

An armless, legless mannequin falls from a tree; a noose cinches around its neck with a snap. It bobs like a dismembered corpse.

Sarah jumps back.

"Nice try! I'm still not scared!"

Something flutters in her peripheral vision. She squints through the trees, detecting a figure fleeing back toward the Garrett house. She sprints after it.

"I'm not sharing my wine with you!" Sarah yells, approaching the back of the house. She slows when she sees Gia through the kitchen window. It looks like she's searching the cupboards and the cabinets.

But if Gia's in there, Sarah wonders, *who am I chasing? Rachel? Couldn't be. She'd never have the guts to pull a prank of this caliber on her own.*

She steps on to the deck and makes her way towards the back door.

In a flash, rusty garden shears rise up between the slats, impaling her foot!

Sarah releases a high-pitched screech, her eyelids fluttering wildly in pain. The blades retract and she falls to the ground. Darkness seems to close in around her as Santa, the demon in red and white, crawls out from under the deck.

He clutches his shears, dripping with fresh blood. He stands in front of the back door, blocking Sarah's path.

Sarah's eyes widen.

The monster charges.

A surge of adrenaline grants Sarah immunity from pain, but not from fear. She scrambles to her feet, blood squirting from her left sole, and races back into the woods. She runs like a woman possessed, like an Olympic marathoner coming down the final stretch.

She breaks branches in her path, leaps rocks—anything to escape from... she knows not what. But she *feels* it, moving quickly and efficiently through the woods behind her, closing in. The Anti-Santa.

Just like her childhood nightmares!

Sarah pushes on, eventually tripping and tumbling into a gulley. Her arms are scraped and bloody; small branches pierce her muscles. The sight makes her want to gag.

Pain setting in, she takes refuge behind a big rock. She braces herself before pulling the finger-sized splinters out of her flesh. Blood squirts across her face. She wants to scream but knows better—knows it will lead the creature straight to her.

She writhes, twitches, and stares at the sky. She gulps air greedily, but quietly. Soon enough, she hears twigs crunching and footsteps approaching.

She tries not to breathe, not to move.

A shadow black as Hades emerges... lingers... and passes.

Sarah waits a few more moments before releasing a silent breath. Ever so cautiously, she peeks over the top of the boulder.

Oh, God!

He's only a few feet away from her, searching through bushes.

Sarah crouches back down, out of sight, feeling numb.

The white-haired killer's head snaps back to the boulder. Yellow, seething eyes spot a few drops of blood in the moonlight.

There! the mask hisses.

Santa circles the rock, but Sarah's gone. Only a fresh puddle of blood remains.

Sarah emerges from the trees, hysterical, confused. She's somehow back in Mrs. Garrett's backyard. Gia's still there in the kitchen! She looks frantically in every direction, scrutinizing every shadow. She takes a couple deep brave breaths, swallows hard, and flies towards the back door.

"Gia!" she screams. "Open the door!" She rushes to the window, palms out, ready to bang on it.

A specter in red and white tackles her from the side like an offensive lineman.

Sarah is being slaughtered. She holds her right hand up to protect her face. Hungry garden shears send all four fingers flying. Blood bubbles and gushes from each stump.

The shears plunge into Sarah's neck, slicing across her windpipe, tearing her jugular.

Blood sprays across the kitchen window as Gia turns toward the living room, and out of sight.

Chapter Twenty-Six

NIGHTMARE BEFORE CHRISTMAS

"**G**randma! Where are you?"

Rachel rushes back into her grandmother's house, leaving Jasper the cat outside. She returns to the dining room and regards the soggy, whiskey-soaked pictures.

"What a mess," she mutters, picking up the pictures a few at a time and shaking them off. She begins to organize them on the tabletop, swirling with emotion; nostalgia, regret, and trepidation.

There are pictures from Rachel's high school graduation; there she is with Gia and Sarah, the trio wearing caps and gowns. There's her prom pictures with Cody; he's wearing a powder blue tuxedo and she's got an ungodly corsage on her wrist.

"Oh, Grandma," she whispers. "Why the hell did you pull these old things out?"

Rachel looks at older pictures from before her mom disappeared, the two of them on a playground, dressed up as hippies, roasting marshmallows over a campfire.

"Mom..." she holds back tears. And then she gasps—her stomach clenches.

It's a picture she's never seen before. A picture of her

mother, kissing—Mr. Garrett! She turns it over; the writing's blurred from the whiskey bath, but it's still legible.

"All my love, now and forever. –PG"

Rachel feels like she just fell through a trap door, like the ground beneath her feet is gone, leaving her careening into nothingness.

Her cell phone rings, snapping her back to reality. Trembling, she answers it without even looking at the caller ID.

"H-hello?" She's in a daze.

"Rachel!" It's Cody. "I'm glad you answered."

Rachel doesn't know how to respond, so she says nothing.

"It was nice to see you this evening," he continues. "I'd like to see you again, if—"

"Cody!" she interrupts, finally regaining her senses.

"Yeah?"

"I'm freaking out!"

"What's wrong?"

"I can't find my grandma," she replies. "And I just found these old pictures of my mom—with Mrs. Garrett's husband!"

"Whoa!" Cody's blown away. "What kind of pictures."

"Pictures that suggest they knew each other—and that they were more than just friends."

"You think your mother was having an affair with Mr. Garrett?"

"It sure looks that way," Rachel replies. "I wonder if Mrs. Garrett knew?"

"Jesus Christ!"

"And there's more! I found out that Mr. Garrett was a monster!"

"What do you mean?"

"I mean he was a wife beater and a child abuser. They locked him up at Readcrest Institute for the Criminally Insane."

"Jesus."

"That's not the worst of it, Cody. I think he broke out last night—I think he escaped!"

"My God!" Cody sounds beside himself.

"He could be out there stalking Mrs. Garrett right now! She left her house a while ago and hasn't come back!"

"Holy shit!" What else can Cody say, really?

"I don't know what to do. I don't know what's going on?"

"Let me hop on the internet and do some research," Cody says.

"Oh my God!" Rachel gasps. "I just realized that Gia could be in danger! I've got to go back to Mrs. Garrett's house!"

Chapter Twenty-Seven

GIA REMMY

Back at Mrs. Garrett's house, Gia returns to the living room with her glass of eggnog. She starts to take a sip—and notices something on the couch. It's a bottle of cheap white wine from Stop and Shop.

The next thing she notices is that the front door is ajar.

"Sarah?" Gia calls. "Are you back?" She picks up the bottle of wine and heads to the door. She opens it wider, and looks up the street. "Sarah?"

No response; only wind and crickets.

"I'm drinking this!" she shouts before going back inside, closing the door behind her. She takes a seat on the couch, placing the bottle of wine and the glass of eggnog on the coffee table.

She pulls out her cell phone and calls Rachel. Her call goes straight to voicemail.

"Hey Rachel, is Sarah with you? Where are you guys? Give me a call when you get this."

As though on a timer, a Ferris wheel music box springs to life, playing a calliope tune.

Gia shudders.

"Where is everybody?" she whispers. She cracks open the wine (a twist-off cap) and takes a hearty swig straight from the bottle. Liquid courage. Feeling fortified, she goes to inspect the spinning Ferris wheel antique.

It sits on an end table in front of a row of Santa mannequins. As she approaches, and unbeknownst to her, one of the Santas turns his head—ever so slowly. Gia is transfixed; she watches the Ferris wheel spin, as she takes another swig of white wine.

"Everything in this house is creepy." She jumps at the sound of soft footsteps upstairs. "Sarah," she calls, moving to investigate. "Are you up there?"

She tentatively mounts the stairs and peers down the dim corridor. The study door is open with small lights flickering from within.

Gia moves delicately down the hallway, unaware she's being followed.

She enters the creepy old study, illuminated by a few flameless candles. She walks to the window and looks outside. Wind whips the treetops.

There's a small sound from behind a closet door, like something falling from a shelf—or someone hiding.

"Sarah?"

She opens the closet door—cautiously, eyes bulging with grim anticipation. The blackness within seems supernatural, almost infinite.

"Sarah," she calls in a childlike cadence. "Come out come out wherever you are."

The closet is empty—but Gia isn't alone. Santa emerges from the shadows behind her.

Gia, hears the shuffling of footsteps at her back. She spins, finding herself in the presence of a not so friendly St. Nick—an abomination in a Santa suit.

Garden shears poised, Santa leaps towards Gia.

She moves instinctually, without thinking. The beast swings as she ducks; he swings again as she grabs a lamp. When he swings for a third time, Gia smashes him in the head, grabs him by the shoulders, and pushes him into the closet.

It turns out, when shit goes down, Gia's a badass.

As Santa struggles to his feet, Gia bolts downstairs, straight towards the front door. She's horrified to discover it's locked. She struggles with the knob and the deadbolt, but it won't budge. She looks up and almost screams.

A new padlock has been installed near the top of the door-frame. Gia tugs at it fiercely but it's locked tight. She hears the mad Santa coming after her from upstairs and pivots, sprinting into the kitchen.

She gasps when she sees a similar padlock on the back door.

"No!" Gia screams.

She turns to the window and struggles to open it but can't. It's sealed shut with long screws. Gia pounds on the glass, frustrated. She grabs a knife from the butcher block on the counter and spins around, expecting to come face to face with death in a red felt cap.

No one's there.

Breathing hard, Gia closes her eyes, wishing she were somewhere else—anywhere else. The house has gone silent, but she knows she can't stand still; she's got to keep moving.

She slinks into the downstairs bathroom and quietly locks the door. Quiet as a mouse, she sets down the knife and inspects a small window above the shower. She attempts to open it, but it won't budge either.

Damn!

There's a slight sound behind her. Gia whimpers as the bathroom doorknob moves... slowly. Gia freezes, trembling, vibrating. The doorknob jiggles harder, then violently—then stops.

Gia bites her lips, sweat and tears run down her face. She waits several long moments before turning back to the window.

Suddenly, the window shatters, showering Gia's face with shards of glass. She screams desperately as a hulking arm reach through, silencing her with a death grip around her throat.

Obliterate her! the mask commands.

Chapter Twenty-Eight

NAUGHTY LIST

Rachel runs out the front door of her grandmother's house, sprinting towards the Garrett house, cell phone pressed against her ear.

"I still don't understand, Cody," she says breathlessly. "Why would my grandma keep all this from me?"

"To protect you," he replies.

Rachel can hear him typing on his laptop.

"From what?" She's overwhelmed and indignant. "The truth?"

"Do you think Mrs. Garrett knew?" Cody asks before specifying. "About her husband and your mom?"

"God, I hope not," Rachel replies. "If she did, I can't imagine why she'd want anything to do with me. I'd be, like, a painful reminder that her husband cheated on her."

"Probably..." Cody continues typing.

"Then again, she did say she had something to tell me when she got home tonight. Why did my mom disappear on the same night Mr. Garrett went to jail. There has to be a connection, right? I mean..." She loses her train of thought when she notices that Mrs. Garrett's car has returned; it's parked in its usual space.

"Here it is!" Cody exclaims. "I've got access to the inmate database for Readcrest."

"And?" Rachel prods. "Is he on it?"

"Yes!" Cody confirms. "He was locked up on an indefinite sentence almost exactly fifteen years ago."

"Oh my God! Mrs. Garrett really is in trouble—we all are!"

"Hold on," Cody says, still typing. "There's an asterisk here, something else about Mr. Garrett. Damn it, dead-link!" Cody sighs. "Let me make a few phone calls and call you right back."

"Thanks, Cody," Rachel replies, suddenly feeling very sorry for the way she had left things with him. "I'm so sorry for—"

"Don't worry about that," he replies. "I'll talk to you soon."

They hang up.

Rachel sees a scrap of paper blowing down the street in her direction. She'd ignore it—except it looks like it's tumbling right towards her—like it wants her to pick it up. It comes in contact against her shoe like it has a mind of its own; Rachel leans down to pick it up.

"What the fuck?" she whispers.

It's a Naughty List.

It's covered with names; some are people Rachel knows, others are acquaintances. She trembles when she sees her friends' names—"Gia Remmy" and "Sarah Blair"—crossed out. The implications are shocking.

She notices another name—her own... only slightly different. Next to "Rachel Kimmel" is a question mark, as though the list's maker has yet to decide her fate.

Knowing that Gia and Sarah are in trouble (or worse), Rachel makes her way past the mob of mannequin Santas and through the front door—which is no longer locked. The living room is bathed in an orange glow from the fireplace. Christmas carols play softly on an old radio, punctuated with static.

"Gia?" Rachel calls. "Sarah?"

The song "Silent Night" playing on the radio is the only reply; in this context, its lyrics feel twisted and ominous.

Rachel creeps towards the fireplace and retrieves the brass poker. She prepares to investigate, but spies Gia's glass of eggnog on the coffee table.

She pulls out her cell phone. She dials Gia's number and presses the phone to her ear. She hears it ringing—from somewhere in the house. Rachel walks to the foot of the stairs and calls up. "Gia? Sarah?"

The call goes to Gia's voicemail.

Rachel hangs up.

Rachel ascends the stairs, slowly, one step at a time. Each step creaks. Once on the landing, she peers down the hallway. There's a flashing light emanating from Jamie's room.

Rachel makes her way inside. She finds Gia's cell phone in the center of Jamie's bed, right beside the rag doll—and a key. She picks up the key. Could it be the one she was looking for earlier?

Her cell phone rings. She pockets the key before answering.

"Cody!" She's nearly breathless.

"Rachel!" He seems frantic too.

"Something's wrong, Cody! I can't find Gia or Sarah anywhere. Mrs. Garrett's car is here, but I can't find her either!"

"Rachel, I found out—"

"It's got to be Mr. Garrett!" She's nearly frenzied. "He's here, somewhere—I can feel it!"

"Hold on!" Cody yells. "Slow down. I need to tell you something!"

"Oh my God!" She shudders. "What if Mr. Garrett did something to my mom before he was sent away? What if he wants to kill me too?"

"No," Cody insists. "Rachel, stop! Listen to me! It's important!" He gets her attention.

"What?"

"Mr. Garrett *died* at Readcrest—ten years ago!"

"What?" Rachel's head spins; her knees tremble. "Then... then who..." She hears noise downstairs, some kind of commotion.

"Cody!" she whispers, panicked. "Someone's here!"

"Rachel? Are you there?"

The low-battery warning on Rachel's cell phone beeps.

"Cody! Help me! I need you! Call the police!"

Her phone loses all power.

Chapter Twenty-Nine

SANTA BABY

Rachel pockets her phone. She uses both hands to hold the brass poker like a baseball bat, like a broad sword. She makes her way down the hallway, and then down the stairs. The house is quiet again, except for the sounds of "White Christmas" now on the old radio.

She dashes to the front door, disheartened to discover an intimidating padlock holding the door to the frame. That wasn't locked before! She turns, bravely venturing towards the back of the house.

She sees something—light coming out from behind the basement door. She reaches into her pocket, retrieves the key, and slides it into the padlock. It's a perfect fit!

Rachel bravely descends the basement stairs, finding the room illuminated by a few flameless candles. She comes off the last step, gripping the fireplace poker tight. The dreary room pulses with palpable grief.

"Oh my God..."

Rotting boxes are everywhere.

Sheets of thick plastic hang down from support beams.

The air is stifling and insufferable; Rachel tries not to breathe.

There's a small metal cage in the corner, barely large enough to comfortably house a terrier. A sign above it reads: *"Time Out."*

Rachel steps in to inspect a wooden table in the center of the room. It's about the size of a door with loose straps attached to each corner. There's a silver tray beside it; a rusty pair of scissors sits atop it, along with a needle and thread. The image is surreal.

"What is this?" she whispers.

The walls are covered with colorful signs: *"Girls Are Pretty." "Girls Love Dolls." "Girls Like Pink."*

Rachel shudders. It hits her like a ton of bricks.

"Oh my God..." Rachel says to herself.

"Yes, dear..."

Rachel turns and sees Mrs. Garrett. Rachel screams.

"I would have told you everything," the old lady says, approaching Rachel slowly. "I wanted to. I tried."

Rachel points the fire poker at her. "Stay away from me!"

"I'm not going to hurt you," she says in a voice that offers little sincerity.

"You weren't protecting Jamie!" Rachel yells. "You were the one abusing her!"

"You've got it all wrong," Mrs. Garrett replies. "Put down the poker, dear."

Upstairs, they hear the sounds of heavy footsteps. Rachel wants to run, but Mrs. Garrett blocks the exit. She yells:

"Cody? Is that you? I'm in the basement! Mrs. Garrett's crazy!"

Mrs. Garrett laughs.

"I assure you, dear," she says emphatically. "That's... not... Cody."

Rachel's body seizes at the implication. She hears the footsteps approaching, purposeful and intent. The floor about them seems to tremble. Whoever's up there, they must be massive.

"It can't be..." Rachel can barely fathom the insanity.

"What's that dear?" Mrs. Garrett replies.

"It can't be your husband..." The walls seem to be melting. "It can't be your husband—he's dead!" Rachel waves the fire poker at her frantically.

Mrs. Garrett chuckles.

The footsteps creep closer, pausing at the basement door before descending. One step at a time, boot over boot, until— the assassin Santa emerges. His face, beyond black, his body nearly herculean.

"Who is that?" Rachel yells. The fireplace poker suddenly feels very heavy in her hands and her head is spinning.

Mrs. Garrett stands beside the grisly slasher.

"Say hello to my daughter—Jamie!"

It's like a bomb goes off in Rachel's brain.

"That's impossible..." Rachel goes limp; her eyes momentarily roll into the back of her head. She falls to the ground, terror-stricken.

"Put her in the chair!" Mrs. Garrett orders.

Santa descends upon Rachel, picks her up like a rag doll, and slams her down in a gaudy antique with sturdy oak armrests. She wilts, seemingly melting under the weight of her own body.

"You're lying to me," Rachel insists, drooling, her head bobbing. "Tell me the truth!"

"Jamie was five-years-old when my husband found out the 'truth'. He was so disgusted that he tried to kill her... put her out of her misery." She laughs. "At least that's what I told the police!"

The Santa in the blacker-than-black mask looms over Rachel, heaving. She's terrified, resigned, and still struggling to put it all together.

"You see..." Mrs. Garrett gives her the final piece of the puzzle. "Jamie was born a filthy, disgusting boy!"

Rachel gasps in horror.

Jamie retreats into a corner, clutching his blood-drenched gardening shears. He looks down at his feet, shifting his weight from side-to-side. The intimidating behemoth suddenly looks very small.

"I was expecting a lovely little girl," Mrs. Garrett continues. "You can imagine my surprise when I gave birth to a manipulating, perverted, womanizing... man! So, when I came home from the hospital, I brought Jamie down here and... fixed the little problem."

Jamie moans quietly. He hides his face behind a red sleeve, ashamed.

"It was as easy as removing a nasty wart."

"You're sick..." Rachel's seeing double and triple. She leans over and pukes. The entire room feels like it's vibrating.

Mrs. Garrett walks slowly towards her.

"After my husband was arrested, Jamie's secret was finally revealed. But, as a battered wife, I convinced everyone that my husband was responsible for the... mutilation."

The depth of Mrs. Garrett's depravity is staggering.

Rachel feels as though she's being consumed by a fever dream. Nightmare piling on top of nightmare, stretching her psyche to the limits of sanity.

"Still, poor Jamie was taken from me," Mrs. Garrett continues, "taken to the Morningstar Center for Troubled Children where she remained—until very recently."

The MCTC has long been tied to as many local urban legends and horror stories as Readcrest. Tales of young wards mistreated at the hands of an uncaring staff are infamous. Children were often subjected to isolation, unnecessary medical procedures—and worse.

Mrs. Garrett looks at Jamie adoringly.

"She just couldn't stay away for Mama," she beams. "She found a way to liberate herself. She's so smart!"

"You'll never get away with this…" Rachel struggles with every word, like an exhausted swimmer lost at sea, treading water. "My friends will save me… we'll call the police… my grandma will…"

Before Rachel can complete the sentence, Mrs. Garrett pulls one of the plastic sheets from a support beam revealing—Abbey's broken and bloody body, pulled up from the depths of the Ravine.

"No!"

Mrs. Garrett pulls down another sheet revealing—Sarah's mutilated body, tossed into the corner like a pile of trash.

"I hate you!"

Mrs. Garrett yanks down the final sheet of plastic revealing—Gia's mangled frame. She's still wearing the female mannequin's sequin dress, blood cascades down her neck.

"Gia…" Rachel groans.

"You know," Mrs. Garrett leans in until she and Rachel are nearly nose to nose. "Your mother spent some time in that cage in the corner." She turns her head to the sign reading *"Time Out."*

"What did you say about my mother?" Tears break through. She hasn't cried in almost fifteen years—until now.

"Oh, you poor dear. Your mother's a filthy whore. She fucked my husband and threatened to expose me to the police."

"Where is she?" Rachel screams. "Tell me!" she begs.

Mrs. Garrett's smile is demonic.

"I buried the bitch in my garden."

It's all too much. The horror's overwhelming, oppressive, suffocating. Unconsciousness, at this point, is a mercy, a blessing.

Rachel slumps forward in the chair as her entire world fades to black.

JINGLE JANGLE

"**D**etective Barker speaking." It's been a relatively quiet night for the Napa Valley Police Department. Quiet but ominous. Most of the officers have the night off, but Barker hasn't been able to shake the feeling that something isn't right.

There have been reports of kids causing mischief of the usual variety, but something sinister seems to be quietly bubbling beneath the surface.

Little Jacob Davenport had been found by neighbors that morning, wandering the streets alone, unable to find his mother. Shiela Davenport wasn't exactly mother of the year, but ducking out on her little boy around Christmas was unfathomable. What was most unnerving, however, was the boys account of "Santa" knocking at his door the night before.

"Detective Barker, this is Deputy Luna," the voice on the phone was hurried, rattled. "We've got a real scene here at the Stop and Shop. Jonathan Curtis is dead!"

"What!" Barker screams into the receiver. "Any witnesses?"

"We're reviewing security tapes now, Sir, but..."

"Well, spit it out, Luna!"

"Sir, someone reported seeing a Santa Claus leaving the scene."

No! His stomach clenches. There'd been about half a dozen calls about the Santa prowler, but this represents a major escalation. He can't afford to stand idly by, waiting for this sicko to strike again. At this point, it's not a matter of "if" but "when."

"We'll have a unit on the scene shortly," he tells Officer Luna. "Hang tight!" He clicks a button on his phone. "Barton! Send a car out to the Stop and Shop—and be on the lookout for Santa Fucking Claus!"

I haven't seen anything like this in thirty-five years, Barker thinks, shaking his head. *Nothing even close. This Santa prowler is one sick motherfucker.*

He calls out loud through his office door for the desk officer on duty.

"Deputy Wong! I'd like to see you."

Wong hustles in, eager to be of service. He's freshly promoted and looking to make a name for himself within the department. He's also one of the few officers who doesn't hate Detective Barker.

"Have you had a chance to plot out all of those Santa prowler sightings on a map?

"Yes, Sir." Wong replies. He rushes out, returning a few seconds later with an ungainly map.

Barker spreads it across his desk; the two lawmen study the string of red dots.

Detective Barker scratches his head. *There's gotta be a connection,* he thinks.

It isn't long before a pattern emerges.

"Looks like a cluster around Spalding Road," Wong notes. "The prowler could even be hiding down in that ravine."

"I was just up on Spalding earlier this evening," Barker recalls. "Had a word with that old bag Mrs. Garrett about that fucked up kid of hers."

"You know," Wong interjects, "growing up, we all used to think Mrs. Garrett was a witch. She used to scare the shit out of us."

Barker chuckles.

"That a fact?"

"You think she's involved?" Wong asks.

"I don't see how," Barker replies. "She doesn't look like she could swat a fly, much less take out a bunch of healthy twenty-year-olds." He lights a fresh cigarette and rubs his chin. "Unless someone's helping her out."

"Sir!" Officer Lowery sticks his head into Barker's office. "We've gotten calls from the parents of Gia Remmy and Sarah Blair. The girls never came home from the mall tonight and they're worried about the prowler."

"Keep me posted, Lowery."

"Yes, Sir," Lowery replies before heading back into the main office.

"Gia Remmy and Sarah Blair," Barker ponders. "They're both friends with that Rachel Kimmel girl, aren't they?" he asks Wong.

"I believe so," the deputy replies.

"And she lives right there on Spalding Road too." His thoughts are spinning.

"Should we send over a few units?" Deputy Wong asks.

"Not yet," Barker replies. "I'm still not sure all of this is connected." He stamps out his cigarette and stands up. He puts his side arm in his shoulder strap and starts putting on his jacket. "Let's take have a look first, then we can assess the situation."

"Yes, Sir," the deputy replies.

"Saddle up, Wong. We're going for a ride."

Chapter Thirty-One
TWO EYES MADE OUT OF COAL

Rachel's eyes snap open and, for a moment, she isn't sure if they're open at all. It's darker than dark, like the core of a black hole. Slowly, the infinite blackness recedes into shades of gray, purple, and brown. After a few more minutes of shaking off her drug-induced daze, she begins to fully comprehend the reality of her predicament.

She's in Jamie's room, on Jamie's bed. She's dressed up like a moppet, like Disney's Alice in Wonderland: a blue dress with puffy white shoulders and a lace underskirt. She's wearing thigh-high socks and shiny black shoes; her hair is in pigtails.

There's a ball-gag in her mouth.

Her hands are tied to the bed frame.

She wishes it were a nightmare—all of it. She wishes she had never come home for Christmas. With her grandmother and friends dead and dismembered, she feels truly alone in this world, and responsible for untold miseries.

It's all my fault.

She doesn't have time to feel too sorry for herself—heavy footsteps are stomping down the hall. Sorrow becomes terror in a heartbeat. A formidable figure stands in the doorway: Jamie, still dressed in his blood-soaked Santa suit.

On instinct, Rachel shuts her eyes and goes limp.

Jamie peeks in, menacing but also seemingly excited, like a little kid who can't wait for his new plaything to wake up.

Jamie grunts and leaves, pacing up and down the hallway. Every minute or so, he pops his head back in to check on Rachel.

When Rachel hears Jamie retreating, she pulls frantically at the straps holding her wrists to each side of the bed. When she hears Jamie approaching, she plays passed-out again. After a few of his passes, she's finally starting to make progress.

She gets her right hand free, but the left one won't budge. She picks at the tight knots with her fingernails, choking behind the ball-gag. She pulls with all her might—a little too hard. She huffs, a tiny puff of exertion—but it's enough for Jamie to hear.

He's suddenly back, hovering in the door frame. He sees that her eyes are open. He's holding his gardening shears like they're his favorite dolly.

Rachel struggles like a wild woman to free herself. Her screams are muffled behind the ball-gag.

Jaime steps into the room.

Rachel feels the bones in her left hand popping and grinding as she tries to escape the binding, but she doesn't stop her efforts.

Jamie looms closer.

Rachel feels like the skin of her hand is about to be ripped off like a tight-fitting glove.

Jamie rushes at her.

In a single motion, Rachel frees herself, nearly crippling her hand in the process. She grabs a pink lamp from the end table. As soon as Jamie's in range, she shatters it across his face. Shards pierce the latex mask, nearly blinding her attacker.

Jamie stumbles back into the hallway.

Rachel jumps off the bed. She hears a ruckus just outside the door; sounds of a struggle followed by a loud *thwack* and a powerful *thud*. Confused and aghast, Rachel retreats under the bed. Once fully hidden, she removes her ball-gag—and waits.

Someone comes back into the room—slowly. Rachel sees black boots creeping around, one leg limping. She closes her eyes, imagining herself invisible.

There's a whisper. "Rachel?"

She whispers back, "Cody! Thank God!"

He helps her out from under the bed. Rachel sees that he's holding a fire extinguisher under his left arm.

"I knocked that colossal maniac out with this," he explains. "Who *is* that?"

Rachel is relieved to see him, but still frantic. "No time to explain!" As if on cue, Jamie comes charging back in. Clearly, Cody's blows were not as debilitating as he thought. "Cody!" she screams. "Look out!"

Jamie grabs Cody, jerks him away from Rachel, and slams him against the wall. Tables are upended, mirrors are shattered, and porcelain dolls fly through the air like rabid seagulls.

Jamie smashes Cody into another wall; plaster cracks and supports splinter. They roll around on the floor. Finally, Jamie picks Cody up over his head and rushes back into the hall. There's a *yowl* and another powerful *thud* followed by excruciating silence.

Rachel whispers, "Cody?" She can't see him. She creeps closer to the door. "Cody are you ok? Cody, please answer me!"

Cody leaps back into the room. Rachel almost screams, but her fear disappears, replaced by relief.

"I think he was trying to do an atomic pile driver on me," Cody says. "But he cracked his head against the wall!"

Rachel peers into the hall. Jamie's in a heap in the hallway, but he's still moving—attempting to get back up.

"We've got to get out of here," she says. "Now!"

"I can't run," Cody tells her. "My leg... I think he stabbed me..."

Indeed, Cody's got a nasty gash running the length of his thigh. It looks hideous, but it could have been much worse. At least Jamie didn't nick any arteries.

"Shit!" Rachel thinks fast. "I know where you can hide. Come on!"

Rachel helps Cody hobble away from Jamie, and into Mrs. Garrett's room. She leans him up against the bed frame and pulls the sexy Santa mannequin off the mattress.

"Lie down!" Rachel tells Cody.

Cody's surveys the sexy Santa with morbid curiosity. "What is that thing?" he asks.

"No time to explain! Lie down! I'm going to cover with you in a sheet. Then all you have to do is lie perfectly still."

Pained and bleeding, Cody does as he's told.

"Don't make a sound," Rachel urges. "And don't come out no matter what. I'll be back for you when it's safe."

"I came here to save you, not the other way around," Cody says. "I wanted to show you how much you mean to me."

Rachel can see the fear and uncertainty in his eyes.

"We're going to get out of this," she tells him. "I promise. And, when I do... maybe there will be another chance for us..."

Cody looks like he's about to cry.

"I'm going to get help," she says in a tone meant to sooth him. "I won't leave you this time. I promise."

They hear footsteps. A shadow approaches. Cody freezes as Rachel pulls the sheets over him. She ducks out of sight behind the bed just as Jamie pops his head in.

Rachel lies flat on her stomach and scurries under the bed. She faces the doorway, putting her hand over her mouth to mute her heavy breath. She's stiff as a board.

Jamie enters the bedroom; his hollow rasping causes every hair on Rachel's body to stand on end. She sees his big black boots creeping. They pause near the edge of the bed.

Above her, Cody's bleeding more than either of them realized. A steady flow of blood trickles onto the hardwood floor.

Suddenly, Jamie reaches under the bed. In an instant he grabs a fistful of Rachel's hair and drags her out, flailing and screaming. He holds her over his head with ease and heaves her against a wall. Rachel crumples into a heap, right below Mrs. Garrett's bedroom window.

She's wracked with pain and terror. She considers going limp and letting Jamie have his way with her. Anything to save Cody.

She gazes through the glass, up at the starry sky. There's a moment of clarity. *I wonder if Mrs. Garrett screwed* all *of her windows shut...*

Mustering all her strength, Rachel gets on her knees and pushes on the window. It opens.

Jamie charges like a bull, snorting and grumbling.

Out of options, Rachel jumps from the second story.

Chapter Thirty-Two

ROCKIN' AROUND THE CHRISTMAS TREE

Rachel lands in the backyard with a *thud*. Several ribs crack and the wind is knocked out of her, but it's better than contending with the maniac in the house. Fighting the urge to fall unconscious again, this time from the pain, Rachel gets to her feet—staggering. She has to decide whether to run for help or go back to rescue Cody. She can hear Jamie inside, moaning as he clambers through the house after her.

He's coming! With some distance between her and her attacker, Rachel's desire to fight suddenly overrides her yearning for flight. She sees a shovel sticking out of the ground beside a row of begonias. She grabs it and scrambles onto the back deck of the house.

Jamie bursts out the back door and onto the deck, his gardening shears thick with coagulating blood. He's seemingly shocked to see Rachel standing firm with her shovel; maybe he expected her to flee into the woods.

They regard one another, sizing up the situation. It's a standoff.

Is this really the same person who used to look down longingly at the other children from a window? Rachel thinks. *Is there anything left of the innocent, uncorrupted soul left?*

Jamie seems poised to strike.

"Jamie!" Rachel says.

The name, and Rachel's voice, stop him in his tracks.

Without warning, there's a flash of lightning and a crack of thunder as the clouds unleash a torrent of rain. They're both drenched in seconds.

"It wasn't your fault, Jamie," she says. "It was your mother. She's the one who hurt you and locked you up like an animal!"

The words appear to confuse Jamie. He slowly lowers his shears.

She's lying! the mask screams. *Cut her in half!"*

Jamie raises his shears again and springs forward, but Rachel is ready for him. She swiftly knocks the shears out of his hands with her shovel. She doesn't want to hurt him, but saving Cody is her first priority. She brings the flat of the shovel down on Jamie's skull with a sickening *clunk.*

Jamie topples over. He remains motionless for several long moments. Rachel stands in the stormy weather, panting until the adrenaline surge relents and she catches her breath.

Cody needs me, she tells herself before heading back inside through the door, still clutching her shovel.

Once inside, she listens. She hears nothing. The house is eerily still. Rachel continues, heel-to-toe, heart pounding. Practically holding her breath, she creeps past the dining room and towards the stairs. She winces at every tiny creak of the floorboards.

Without warning, Mrs. Garrett walks swiftly past her and into the living room. It's a miracle she didn't see Rachel standing there, drenched to the bone, clutching a shovel. Mrs. Garrett is standing before a row of Santas, addressing them.

"I can't thank you all enough for showing me the true meaning of Christmas," she gushes.

Rachel continues towards the staircase.

"I know these past few years have been hard on all of us," Mrs. Garrett tells the Santas. "But those sad days are over. Jamie's home, and now that we have Rachel—"

Rachel takes another cautious step, but it's no good. A floorboard creaks. Mrs. Garrett turns around like a raptor, and immediately rushes toward Rachel.

"Where do you think you're going?" she screams. Before Rachel can even react, Mrs. Garrett pulls a clear plastic bag over Rachel's head and tightens it around her neck.

Rachel reflexively drops her shovel. She can't believe how strong this seemingly fragile old lady is. It's like Mrs. Garrett is possessed by a demon. Rachel claws at her own throat and tries to tear holes in the plastic but she can't. She's fading fast.

Like a professional wrestler, Mrs. Garrett drags Rachel back to the dining room and throws her on the table. Tepid bowls of Christmas stew and fine China hit the walls and the floor, crashing around them.

Rachel, the plastic bag around her neck, fumbles for something to fight with, but only comes up with a salad fork. She rolls off the table and crouches like a samurai, holding the fork out for protection.

Mrs. Garrett looks down at her, smiling, unafraid.

"What are you going to do with that, dear?" she asks. "Eat some baby greens?" She's so pleased with her own joke, she raises her head and laughs.

Rachel pulls the plastic bag off of her head.

"Eat this!" she yells. She lunges, and brings the fork down into Mrs. Garrett's right foot.

Shrieking with pain, Mrs. Garrett launches at Rachel. The two grapple across the walls, essentially tearing the entire room apart, each vying for the upper hand.

Rachel stumbles upon a random mannequin arm. It's not her first choice for a weapon, but it's better than a salad fork. She grabs it, and swings it at Mrs. Garrett, delivering a swift uppercut that sends the old lady spinning.

Mrs. Garrett's arms windmill as she struggles for balance before falling over on her face.

Rachel stands over the old woman and raises the mannequin arm high above her head. She aims at Mrs. Garrett's face.

"This is for my mother!" she screams.

Jamie suddenly bursts into the dining room from the kitchen; he's soaking wet and apoplectic. He throws himself between them, and grabs Rachel in a bear hug while his mother gets to her feet.

Rachel struggles in Jamie's grasp and loses her grip on the mannequin arm. Mrs. Garrett collects herself, blood dribbling down her forehead.

"Now you've done it," she says to Rachel, her words pure poison. "Now, you've gone and pissed me off." She bends down and picks up the errant mannequin arm. She saunters up to Rachel, burning with rage.

"I owe you one," she says before slamming the arm down on top of Rachel's head.

The pain is incredible; Rachel's ears are ringing. Clouds close in from her peripheral vision and become a tunnel. She's blacking out again. The last thing she hears before losing consciousness is Mrs. Garrett's voice.

"Take her back to the basement!"

Chapter Thirty-Three

YOU'RE A MEAN ONE

Rachel slowly regains consciousness. She's still weak, reeling, and confused. She's back in Mrs. Garrett's terrifying basement, seated in the same chair.

The rag doll sits in her lap. Her wrists are tied.

Rachel's eyelids are unnaturally heavy. The room is still spinning, flickering with the glow of flameless candles. Everything seems distorted, playing out in slow motion. She senses figures in the periphery, but can't focus.

A sweet voice calls her name.

"Rachel."

Rachel sees a shadowy form before her; slowly it begins to crystalize.

"I've missed you so much, Bunny."

"Mom?" Rachel whispers.

"Be strong." Laura Kimmel smiles. She looks exactly how Rachel remembers her—exactly like she did on the day she disappeared. "I'm right here."

"Mommy?" That's when Rachel is hit with a bucket of ice water. The shock brings her fully back from unconsciousness.

Her mother is gone and Mrs. Garrett stands in her place, holding an empty bucket, upturned and dripping.

"Mommy!" Mrs. Garrett teases. "Mommy!"

Rachel shivers, sinking into despair.

Rachel notices that the basement dungeon has been rearranged. Abbey, Sarah, and Gia have been redressed in intentionally ugly Christmas Sweaters. Their bloody and broken bodies have been propped up on a couch together. Wires stretch their mouths into wide, unnatural smiles. Glasses of eggnog have been super-glued into their cold, dead hands.

"Oh my God!" Rachel screams.

There's a body strapped to the rectangular table, covered in a sheet. Whoever it is, they're still alive, struggling against the ties binding their wrists and ankles. Muffled grunts suggest the person is gagged.

Rachel hopes it isn't who she thinks it is.

Jamie, the horrifying masked Santa, paces nervously around the room.

Mrs. Garrett approaches objects on a medical tray beside the table.

"Your mother had the nerve to threaten me," she tells Rachel while examining the instruments on her tray. "It was the same night my husband and Jamie were taken away. She had the audacity to come into my house!" Mrs. Garrett loses herself in the memory.

"Peter told me everything!" Laura screams, pushing her way into the foyer.

"Leave me alone!" Mrs. Garrett hollers back.

"He told me how crazy you are," Laura says. "He told me what you did to Jamie. You won't get away with it!"

"It wasn't me," Mrs. Garrett lies through crocodile tears. "It was Peter!"

"Bullshit!" Laura replies. "I'll tell the cops everything! You'll be locked up at Readcrest!"

"No," Mrs. Garrett weeps.

"And when you're gone," Laura says, "Peter and I will finally be together. Like we've always wanted to be. We'll be a family with Rachel and Jamie. We'll all get the lives we deserve!"

Mrs. Garrett grabs a twelve-inch Santa Claus figurine and smashes it over Laura's head. Laura collapses to the ground like a pile of old laundry.

"So, you see," Mrs. Garrett says to Rachel, as though her prisoner *had* actually seen her memories. "Your mother didn't leave me any choice, really. Once the hoopla over Peter and Jamie died down, I slit her throat and buried her beneath my roses!"

"No!" Rachel screams. "Mommy!" she howls. All these years, she wanted answers; she wanted the truth. Now, the unfathomable, crushing weight of the truth was like a freight train.

"I'm your Mommy now," Mrs. Garrett replies with the voice of a demon.

"You'll never get away with this!" Rachel says. "The police will find you!"

Mrs. Garrett laughs, deep and satisfied. She walks to a corner of the rectangular table and grabs an end of the sheet.

"Don't count on it," she says, pulling the sheet away, revealing—Cody, stripped down to his boxers and muzzled with a ball-gag. His face is bruised and his nose is bloodied. His swollen eyes look towards Rachel, pleading.

"Oh my God, Cody!" Rachel screams "What are you doing with him? Let him go!"

"I think you need an attitude adjustment," Mrs. Garrett announces. "Jamie! Put her in the time out cage!"

Jamie descends upon Rachel; the infinite blackness of his mask is dizzying. With little effort, he unties Rachel and transfers her into the metal cage. He slams the lid and bolts it shut.

"Let me out of here!" Rachel yells, still clutching the rag doll.

Mrs. Garrett laughs and taunts, but Jamie seems subdued, uncertain. Rachel notices this shift in dynamics.

"Jamie!" Rachel yells, catching the rogue Santa off guard, his eyes narrowing. "Your mom's crazy! Help us!" she pleads. "Help us and we'll help you!"

"I'm the only one who can help you, Jamie," Mrs. Garrett interjects, donning purple surgical gloves. "Come to Mama, darling." Mrs. Garrett holds her hand out to her hideous creation.

"Don't you remember me, Jamie?" Rachel pushes. "I gave you this doll," she holds the doll up again.

Jamie tilts his head... remembering.

"Jamie!" Mrs. Garrett shrieks, startling Jamie who flinches at her tone. "Come to Mama right this instant!"

Reluctantly, Jamie stands by Mrs. Garrett's side. Together, they lord over Cody, gazing silently as the boy struggles fruitlessly. Mrs. Garrett removes his ball gag.

"Leave him alone!" Rachel screams from the time out cage.

"What are you going to do with me?" Cody asks, blood and saliva dribbling down his chin, onto his neck. Panic sweeps over him. "What the fuck are you going to do to me?"

"I promised Jamie that, once the Doctors fixed her brain, I'd fix her body," Mrs. Garrett explains.

Jamie quivers with anticipation, softly hooting like a primate.

"Yes, my dear," Mrs. Garrett responds to Jamie by stroking

the side of his mask. "It's time," she smiles. "Show me what you brought me."

Jamie shuffles off to a corner, returning with his sack. It's bloody and dripping. He retrieves the bag's contents and arranges his "collection" in a line, right there on the table beside Cody.

"Oh my," Mrs. Garrett beams. "You've been busy!"

There's a long one and a short one; a wide one and a pink one. One even has a cute little star tattoo on it.

Cody and Jamie watch in horror; the mother and son laugh like conspirators.

"It's nice to have options, I suppose." Mrs. Garrett picks up Beth's dildo. "Although this one, I'm afraid, will not do." She tosses the hot pink phallus at Rachel; it bounces off the cage and into a corner.

"Have you decided which one you want?" Mrs. Garrett asks Jamie.

Jamie regards his options carefully before shaking his head. He points at Cody's face, then slowly brings his finger down to the boy's crotch.

Cody seizes, breaking out into a cold sweat.

"Oh yes," Mrs. Garrett replies to Jamie. "I had a feeling you'd want the freshest one!"

"Don't you touch him," Rachel yells from her cage, ineffectually shaking the bars."

Nearly petrified, Cody struggles against his straps, to no avail.

"What the hell is going on?" He begins to hyperventilate. "What are you people doing with me?"

"Leave him alone!" Rachel begs. She's overcome with guilt. First, she'd broken Cody's heart and now—now he's facing dismemberment and worse.

I told him to come here, she thinks. *It's all my fault! He'd be better off if he'd never met me!*

"Jamie!" Mrs. Garrett barks. "Put your shears on the table and go get my surgical bag out from under my bed!"

Jamie obediently sets his weapon on the table and goes upstairs.

Once the mutilated man-child is out of earshot, Mrs. Garrett breaks out into another fit of diabolical laughter.

Rachel and Cody exchange terrified looks.

"Don't worry," Mrs. Garrett tells her prisoners after composing herself. "I know Jamie is crazy as a hoot!"

Look who's talking, Rachel thinks.

"I know there's no way I can undo what I did with a little old needle and some thread." She shakes her head, momentarily looking off into space. "No, the only way I can fix Jamie, is with this..." She reaches into her deep red pockets and produces— a gun!

"Let us go, you lunatic!" Cody screams.

Mrs. Garrett ignores him.

"You're insane!" Rachel screams.

"Insane," Mrs. Garrett replies, "would be trying to turn my darling baby girl back into a man!" She turns to look at Rachel, her eyes darkening. "Why on God's green earth would I want to do that?" She pushes her gun back into her pocket and picks up Jamie's rusty garden shears. "The only men worth having... are smooth!" She turns back to Cody, crazed and seething.

Cody's rattled to the core. His eyes are bugging.

Mrs. Garrett uses the rusty garden shears to cut Cody's boxers away in a single swipe.

"You'll never get away with this!" Rachel tries to distract Mrs. Garrett away from Cody. "The cops will figure it out! Everything leads back to you!"

"Ha!" Mrs. Garrett scoffs. "I fooled the cops once. I can fool them again! In fact, they stopped by earlier this evening to tell me Jamie had escaped. But, of course, I already knew that."

"They'll never believe you, you manipulative liar!" Rachel will say anything to keep Mrs. Garrett's attention off Cody.

"What's not to believe?" Mrs. Garrett replies. "My crazy child escapes from a mental institution, kills a bunch of horny hot-bodies, then comes home to try and kill me." The old lady beams with narcissistic joy. "It's ironclad!" Her face switches from wicked to innocent. "I didn't want to kill my only child, officers," she mimes. "I didn't have any choice." She pretends to cry. "It was self-defense..." She looks at the ground and back up again. "They should give me a freakin' Oscar!" She struts over to Rachel's cage. "I'll be a hero!" she says assuredly. "And *we* will live happily ever after!"

"Happily ever after?" Rachel says. "What the fuck are you talking about?"

"You'll be safe here with me." She squats in order to speak to Rachel at eye-level. "I'll never let a man hurt you, or take advantage of you, or lie to you." She looks at Rachel with genuine tenderness. "Not even an innocent child is safe out there." Mrs. Garrett stands up, holding back tears. "I'll protect you, Rachel, just like I tried to do for Jamie—before Peter and your slut mom got in the way." She turns on a dime, mean again. "Which reminds me..."

Mrs. Garrett releases a primal yowl as she rushes Cody. His screams are blood curdling.

With a quick snip, Cody's penis is gone. It almost jumps off his body, ejecting blood like a bottle rocket.

"Cody!" Rachel screams.

Mrs. Garrett doesn't stop there. She plunges the rusty shears into Cody's body maniacally, haphazardly, tearing organs and severing arteries. The level of overkill is astonishing. Before long, Cody's nearly decapitated, his entrails are sliding out from his body cavity and onto the basement floor.

"Why?" Rachel wails. "Why? Why?"

Mrs. Garrett's violent outburst slows then stops. She's

drenched with blood, gasping for breath. Bits of Cody (his left ear, his right nipple, a chunk of his pancreas) are embedded in her clothes and hair.

She looks like she's just had the most amazing orgasm of her life.

"Why?" Rachel weeps. "Why are you punishing me?"

"I'm not punishing you," Mrs. Garrett insists, returning to the cage to give Rachel her full attention. "This is how things were *supposed* to be!"

"What the fuck does that mean?" Rachel replies.

"Peter wasn't just some married man that your lonely single mother had an affair with."

"What?"

"Peter Garrett—is your father, dear."

Rachel almost faints; it's simply too much for her to process.

"That bastard got your mother pregnant the same time he knocked me up. And wouldn't you know it," she shakes her head gingerly. "He gave that bitch a baby girl."

"No..." Rachel moans.

"That's right, dear," Mrs. Garrett insists. "You were supposed to be mine. You and Jamie are sisters. Isn't that right, Jamie?"

Jamie appears at the bottom of the stairs with Mrs. Garrett's surgical bag in hand.

"Jamie, dear," Mrs. Garrett turns to face him. "Were you listening in on Mama's conversation?"

Jamie says nothing. He looks away from his mother and towards Rachel.

"Jamie!" Rachel holds the rag doll up. "Remember, Jamie? I tried to be your friend, didn't I?"

Jamie is confused and agitated, growling and grunting.

Mrs. Garrett senses things are on the verge of spinning out of control; the strict emotional ties she forged with Jamie are loosening. Jamie isn't a child anymore. She walks over and takes the surgical bag out of Jamie's hand.

"Jamie," she says, "Before your operation, I'd like a word with you upstairs—in private." She nudges him up the stairs.

Jamie hangs his head and moves up the stairs, as though he has no choice in the matter.

Before following him, Mrs. Garrett beams at Rachel.

"You and I will be so happy together. I'll finally have the daughter I've always wanted."

Chapter Thirty-Four

O HOLY NIGHT

In the living room, "O Holy Night" plays on the old radio, smattered with static.

Mrs. Garrett is drenched in blood and human debris. Her hair is so frazzled, it looks like she's been electrocuted.

She leads Jamie to the Christmas tree, beckoning him to kneel and behold the presents.

"They're all for you, dear," Mrs. Garrett explains. "I got you something every year you've been away. I always knew you'd come home... eventually."

Jamie I in awe, overwhelmed and overflowing with emotions. He picks up one of the wrapped boxes, holds it to his ear, and shakes it... trying to guess what's inside—like a child. He grabs another, becoming gleeful. It's like he's being given his entire childhood back all at once. He makes sweet, happy noises.

Mrs. Garrett reaches into her pocket, retrieving her gun. She aims it at Jamie's head, but the poor son of a bitch is too rapt in his presents to notice. She's *almost* ashamed of herself. But she's closer to her dream now than she's ever been before. There's no turning back.

"I'm sorry, Baby," she says softly. "It's just that... you no longer belong in this world."

Jamie turns and looks up at his mother, confused.

She keeps the barrel of the gun on Jamie's head, right in the center of that malignant darkness surrounding his wild eyes.

"I only did what I did to protect you," she says. "I thought I could save you and... make you better. I never wanted to you become... this!"

Jamie just stares, befuddled, eyes narrowing within the infinite blackness. He reaches for his mother, whining like a dog.

What the fuck is this bitch doing? the mask hisses.

"Oh Jamie..." A tear falls down her bloody face smeared with makeup. "I really do love you. I just wish you had come back to me like the little girl I remember." She cocks her gun. "After all these years, I finally get to see you again, and... you ain't nothing but a dickless man!"

"Mama?" Jamie speaks. His voice is meek and hoarse.

Fuck You! the mask hisses.

Like the cold-hearted snake she is, Mrs. Garrett takes her shot. There's a flash, a puff of smoke, and a powerful blast.

Jamie lunges right as she pulls the trigger, taking the bullet in his upper torso. He howls in pain.

Mrs. Garrett struggles, managing to get another shot off, which strikes Jamie in the shoulder. She tries to shoot again, but Jamie throws himself at her; they hit the wall together with a thud, knocking framed pictures off and cracking plaster.

Mrs. Garrett manages to smack Jamie in the face with the butt of her gun. He loses his grip on her. She strikes again, nearly fracturing his skull. Blood's trickles out of Jamie's black nose, dribbling over his white mustache.

Mrs. Garrett gets another shot off, hitting Jamie in the stomach above his navel.

The beast is too angry to feel any more pain. He slaps the gun out of his mother's hand and roars.

Mrs. Garrett reaches for her Hail Mary: the retractable knife she keeps hidden in her brassiere. She depresses a button and the blade appears as if by magic, gleaming with Christmas cheer. As Jamie falls upon her, she buries the blade in his back.

Her own child, her own flesh and blood—betrayed.

Jamie howls in horror, rearing back like a wounded grizzly bear—the blade still lodged in his back.

Mrs. Garrett can't believe how powerful Jamie is.

"Jamie," she pleads. "I didn't mean it. Mommy loves you!"

Let's kill this fucking bitch! the mask says in a merciless voice.

Mrs. Garrett drops to her hands and knees, crawling across the hardwood floor, scrambling for the gun. Jamie grabs her leg, but she pulls free, kicking him in his punctured gut in the process.

"Die!" Jamie screams.

He tackles his mother, falling on top of her like an avalanche. They both scream as he climbs further on top of her. She's nearly buried beneath him.

Mrs. Garrett tries to buck him off, but she can't.

Jamie, immensely stronger than his mother, continues to claw and thrash relentlessly.

Mrs. Garrett struggles to get the gun, but Jamie flips her over and straddles her.

He grabs her by the throat and squeezes like an anaconda.

Mrs. Garrett sees the gun and reaches for it; her fingertips swipe the butt. She almost has it!

A foot stomps down, crushing Mrs. Garrett's hand. It's Rachel.

Mrs. Garrett's eyes bug out of her head as her oxygen-deprived brain starts shutting down.

Rachel glares down at the helpless woman without a shred of sympathy.

Jamie looks to Rachel without releasing his hold on Mrs. Garrett's neck.

The siblings make eye contact.

Rachel nods her head.

"Finish her," she says.

A slow rendition of "Come All Ye Faithful" begins playing on the radio.

Mrs. Garrett's body jerks and shudders. Her eyes roll up into her head. Foam gathers at the corners of her mouth.

Rachel sits on the couch and watches calmly as Jamie finishes the job.

Mrs. Garrett convulses, kicking. She knocks over the Christmas tree, sending presents and ornaments flying about the room. Her neck twists like a contortionist for a moment until— she falls limp, completely still.

Jamie removes his hands from around his mother's neck. Even his evil mask falls silent in the presence of Mrs. Garrett's dead body.

For a while, nobody moves.

Eventually, Rachel stands and walks over to Jamie. She puts a hand gently on his shoulder.

Jamie looks up at her. He pauses for a moment before reaching up and slowly pulling off his mask.

Far from the grotesque visage she had imagined, Jamie's face is innocent, youthful—almost curious. Rachel notices that their hair is the same color and texture. They look at each other with a sense of wonder and familiarity.

"We both have our father's eyes," Rachel says.

She'll always mourn her grandmother, her girlfriends, and Cody. Living with their memory won't be easy—especially around Christmas. But locking Jamie up wouldn't help her now.

"Everything that happened," Rachel tells him in a soothing voice, "is her fault." She points at Mrs. Garrett's dead body. "Now she's gone, and I'm not going to let anyone hurt you again —ever."

A tear rolls down Jamie's face.

Rachel rubs his cheeks, tenderly.

They hear the siren of a police car, in the distance, growing louder.

Jamie reaches down and puts the cursed black Santa mask over Mrs. Garrett's bloated face.

"Come on," Rachel says, helping Jamie to his feet. "Let's go home."

Chapter Thirty-Five

VIVIAN GARRETT

Detective Barker brings his car to a screeching halt in front of Mrs. Garrett's house on Spalding Road. He flips off the siren as he and Deputy Wong open their doors and lean out, guns drawn.

Rachel's still dressed as a little girl; Jamie's wrapped in a fresh, clean blanket. They're sitting on the front porch, looking calm and spent. Rachel smokes a cigarette as Jamie rests his weary head in her lap, his face obscured behind a mop of tangled hair.

Barker and Wong holster their weapons and approach with caution.

"There's been a lot of commotion in the neighborhood tonight," Detective Barker says as they saunter forward. "Are you guys... okay?"

They don't respond.

"Rachel Kimmel," Barker says with a bit more authority. "What the hell is going on here?"

"She's inside, officers," Rachel says, deadpan, taking a drag off her cigarette.

"Who is?" Barker asks, confused.

"Mrs. Garrett," Rachel replies. "She was the Santa prowler this whole time. We found her in a bloody Santa suit."

"Holy shit," Barker replies, shaking his head in stunned bewilderment.

"She killed my grandma," Rachel continues. "And my friends Gia and Sarah too. And Cody. They're all in the basement."

Baker and Wong look at Rachel dumfounded.

"Did you hear me?" she yells. "Mrs. Garrett's the Santa prowler, assholes! It was her!"

Barker still can't believe what he's hearing.

"Wong," he barks, "Go check it out."

"Yes, Sir," Wong responds, drawing his weapon and slowly heading inside.

Barker puts his hands on his hips.

"If Mrs. Garrett's the Santa prowler, and a serial killer to boot, that probably means..."

Rachel finishes his thought for him. "That her husband was innocent? That you locked up the wrong person? That you fucked up royally?"

Barker shakes his head, muddled and mortified. He finally acknowledges the man sitting beside Rachel.

"Who might this be?" he asks.

"This is Jamie Garrett," Rachel informs him, still stroking her half-brother's hair lovingly. "There's no need to take him back to the asylum. He's going to live with me from now on."

"Well," Barker hesitates. "I don't know if that's exactly... kosher."

"I'm his next of kin," Rachel replies. "We're related. DNA tests will confirm it."

Jamie sits up, stunned and overwhelmed.

Rachel pulls him close for a hug and whispers into his ear.

"I know you didn't mean to do those terrible things," she says. "I know how good you are deep down."

Jamie coos, tears of joy streaming down his cheeks.

"We've got to stick together," Rachel tells Jamie. "We're all we've got. We're family."

"And you're certain," Barker butts in, "that he had nothing to do with anything that's been happening around here?"

"Is he dressed up like Santa Claus and covered with blood?" Rachel asks sarcastically.

"Well, I'll be…" Barker scratches his head. "Ain't this one for the books." He pulls a cigarette out of his jacket pocket and lights it.

"By the way," Rachel says as she and Jamie stand up. "You'll find my mom's body buried beneath the rose bushes out back."

Detective Barker is out of words. He's simply flabbergasted.

"You're only fifteen years too late to be a hero. Come on Jamie," Rachel says, leading her half-brother off the porch. "Let's go."

The siblings walk slowly down the street, leaning on each other for support.

"Detective Barker!" Deputy Wong rushes back outside, frantic. He's loud enough to get Rachel and Jamie's attention, and they turn back. "Detective Barker! Oh my God, oh my God…"

"Calm down, Wong!" Barker says. "What the hell are you going on about?"

"She's still alive!" Wong yells, almost shrieks. "Mrs. Garrett's still alive!"

Rachel and Jamie's blood runs cold.

"Her pulse is really faint," Wong continues, "but she's alive!"

"Call an ambulance!" Detective Barker commands.

Epilogue

DO THEY KNOW IT'S CHRISTMAS?

One year later...

Mrs. Vivian Garrett resides in an adult care facility west of Modesto. She's been in a persistent vegetative state since the events of last Christmas. Jamie may not have broken his mother's neck as he intended, but he gave her brain a nice long nap.

There's a feeding tube in Mrs. Garrett's stomach and she's intubated; a noisy machine breathes for her. Electrodes on her fingers lead into computers that monitor her heart-rate and blood pressure; they beep and click, producing a monotonous arrhythmic polyphonic dirge.

The facility's decent. Nothing fancy, mind you, but it's better than Mrs. Garrett deserves. The staff is overworked but attentive. Doctors look in on her once or twice a week; they almost universally agree that she's too far gone to ever come back again.

But even the remotest possibility of Mrs. Garrett returning to the land of the living is enough to keep Rachel up nights. She had to drop out of UC Santa Cruz in order to attend to her grandmother's passing and to focus on her brother. Life's hard, but they're making it work—and it's worth it.

Jamie's been progressing beyond what anyone might have hoped for, or even imagined. He never actually suffered from Bowen's Disease, or a cleft pallet, or albinism, or frontonasal dysplasia, or any other illness Mrs. Garrett had claimed. Hours of intensive speech therapy have really paid off; a regime of healthy foods and exercise keeps him fit and focused.

He's even seeing specialists regarding his mutilation. There are some exciting possibilities on the horizon, including regrowing the organ in a lab using his own body tissue. In the meantime, he's slowly acclimating to human contact that doesn't hurt. He can offer pleasure and, just as importantly in his case, he can receive it. Sex is about more than just genitals, after all.

He wears his hair short and combed. He dresses in clothes that match his body *and* his identity. He's tidy and gentle with boyish charm. Many women (and men) find him captivating.

He still has nightmares, though. Rachel does too. Nightmares that'll probably never go away. That's why the siblings have decided to face their fears head-on in a way no one might have predicted: by paying Mrs. Garrett a visit.

The nurses and orderlies smile curiously at the couple as they enter room A13. Mrs. Garrett's never had visitors before. They forgot to sign-in at the front desk, but no one noticed or seems to care.

They close the door. It's not unusual for family and friends to want some privacy.

Inside, the siblings flank Mrs. Garrett.

She's degraded significantly since their last encounter. She's thin—almost skeletal. Her skin's waxy and covered in red and brown blotches. She's almost bald with only tangled wisps of kinky white hair.

Her chest heaves when the machine bangs. Monitors beep

and click like alien insects. A tube feeds her a steady stream of mush and a catheter collects her urine.

"Hello, Mrs. Garrett," Rachel says, lighting a cigarette. It's a filthy habit and it certainly isn't allowed in a medical facility, but no one's around to stop her. "The doctors say you probably won't ever wake up. They say it'll be a miracle if you do."

Jamie looks down at his mother and shakes his head.

"They also told us that you might be able to hear our voices," Rachel continues. "They say you might even understand where you are and what happened to you. The Napa police would still *love* to hear your side of the story, if you ever do decide to... wake up."

Jamie laughs, still tentative about using his words.

"So what do you say, Mrs. Garrett?" Rachel leans closer towards the withering woman, blowing smoke in her sunken face. "Think you're capable of a miracle? I bet you'd just love to tell the cops *your* side of the story. Maybe see the two of us shipped up to Readcrest."

Jamie hums and sighs, shifting his weight from one foot to the other. He's dealing with his emotions remarkably well. A lesser man would tear the bitch to shreds on sight. But Jamie is civilized.

"Well," Rachel says, stomping her cigarette out on the floor. "If you do decide to come back to us, Mrs. Garrett, Jamie and I will be sure to pay you another visit."

"Visit," Jamie replies, nodding in agreement.

"Jamie's come a long way, you depraved psychopath," Rachel says. "You wouldn't even recognize him." She beams at her brother and he smiles brightly back at her. "He's nothing like he was and, more importantly, he's nothing like you."

"Nothing like you!" he reiterates.

"If you can hear us," Rachel says, smiling, "I want you to know that we inherited your house. It turns out you also owned about fifty acres of the woods behind the property. Did you even know that?"

No reply from Mrs. Garrett; just the pumping of oxygen and the beeping of machinery.

"We're gonna tear your creepy fucking house down and turn the entire area into a year-round wilderness camp."

Jamie claps his hands and nods.

"It'll be a safe, inclusive place," Rachel continues. "A place where anyone who's struggling can get the help they need."

"Beautiful!" Jamie says.

"Well, that's about it, Mrs. Garrett," Rachel reaches into her purse. "There's just one more thing. We got you something." She pulls out a small box wrapped in festive paper, topped with a bow. A tag reads: *"To Mrs. Garrett/Mom."* Rachel sets it on the old woman's bed. "Consider this a *new* Christmas tradition."

Jamie chuckles.

"Oh, I'm sorry," Rachel says sarcastically. "Did you need me to open this for you, Mrs. Garrett? Well, of course. I'd be happy to!" She tears through the paper, tossing it on the floor. She opens the cardboard box and reveals—the evil, blacker-than-black Santa mask!

The rhythmic pumping of the ventilator, the random beeps and clicks of the machinery seem to come into focus for a moment. There's a steady beat and a hint of a melody.

"Merry Christmas, Mrs. Garrett." Rachel looks across the bed. "Merry Christmas, Jamie."

"God bless us," Jamie replies.

The siblings depart, leaving the hideous mask on Mrs. Garrett's decrepit chest.

As they exit, the mask, though lifeless and inert, seems to be sucking the light and life right out of the room...

"Merry Christmas," it whispers.

The following pages feature images from the film *All Through the House*. Used by permission.

ALL THROUGH

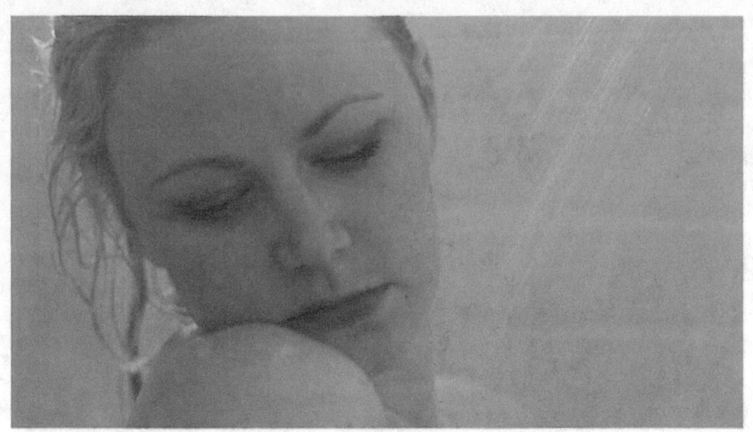

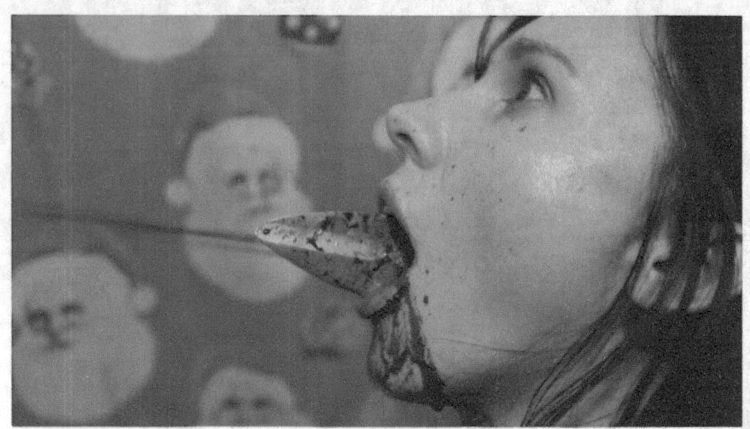
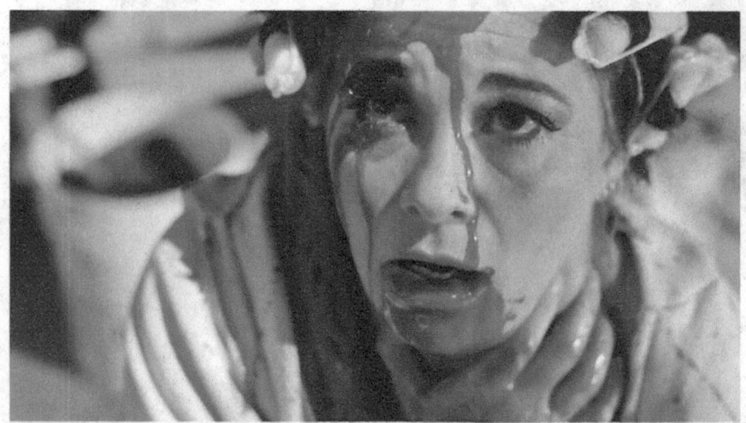

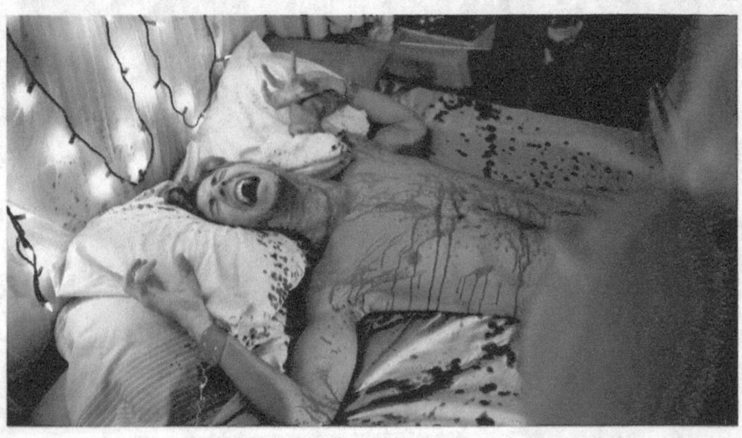

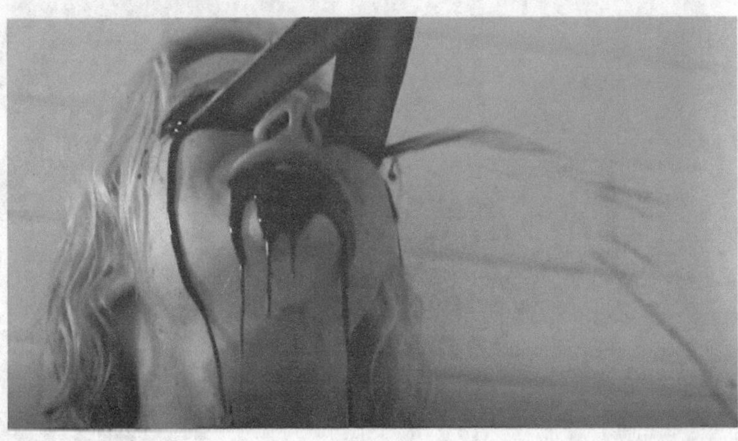

ALL THROUGH THE HOUSE

About the Author

Photo credit: Ama Lea

Over the past decade-plus, Joshua Millican has proven himself to be a horror expert of the highest caliber. After establishing a personal blog in 2011, Millican quickly bccame one of the horror genre's premiere journalists, contributing to many websites before ultimately landing at Dread Central in 2016. One of the top horror outlets on the planet, Millican served as Editor-in-Chief from 2019 through 2021. In addition to writing, Millican has been a member of numerous festival juries, a popular podcast guest, and has even scored a handful of acting gigs. His talk show *Chronic Horror* (sidelined by the Pandemic) explored the intersection of horror movie fandom and cannabis culture. Now married and a father for the first time, Millican pens hardcore horror/sci-fi/fantasy fiction like *Deeper Than Hell* and novelizations like *Forbidden Zone*.

Follow Joshua Millican on Twitter at @josh_millican.